D1380785

'I haven't *asked* you to explain anything,' Briony reminded him.

'No. Unlike most women I know, you're strangely lacking in curiosity.'

'Not really,' she admitted. 'I just don't feel it's any of my business.'

'When I first walked into your shop and saw you,' Teale went on, still speaking musingly, 'the first thing that struck me was the likeness. And I thought, oh, God, no, not again. There can't be two in the world like that.' For a moment, there was such pain in his voice that Briony looked wonderingly at him. 'Those enormous blue eyes, the red curls, same shaped face. But there, thank God, I'm beginning to believe, the resemblance ends.'

'I remind you of someone?' It wasn't hard to deduce. 'Who?'

'My wife, my ex-wife. Charlene.'

Books you will enjoy
by ANNABEL MURRAY

A PROMISE KEPT

Pippa thought she didn't know the Portuguese cousin, Carlos de Alvares, whom her father told her had arrived in England to invite her to visit the mother she hadn't seen for thirteen years. But when she saw Carlos she realised they had met, years ago when she was sixteen and afraid...

GIFT BEYOND PRICE

'Five foot twelve', with a degree in stonemasonry, Laurie Keen wasn't quite the daughter her mother would have liked. However, her future seemed well mapped out—until Curtis Fenton erupted into her world, a cynical journalist who didn't believe in love. Yet there was a spark between him and Laurie that both of them found irresistible...

HEART'S TREASURE

Jacques Fresnay's involvement in the Peruvian expedition came as a surprise to Rylla. Equally surprising was the fact that he seemed to be a genuinely charming and kind man. Yet he had ridiculed her father's work. Did she abide by family loyalty, or give in to Jacques' charm?

COLOUR THE SKY RED

BY

ANNABEL MURRAY

MILLS & BOON LIMITED
ETON HOUSE   18-24 PARADISE ROAD
RICHMOND   SURREY   TW9 1SR

All the characters in this book have no existence outside the imagination of the Author, and have no relation whatsoever to anyone bearing the same name or names. They are not even distantly inspired by any individual known or unknown to the Author, and all the incidents are pure invention.

All rights reserved. The text of this publication or any part thereof may not be reproduced or transmitted in any form or by any means, electronic or mechanical, including photocopying, recording, storage in an information retrieval system, or otherwise, without the written permission of the publisher.

This book is sold subject to the condition that it shall not, by way of trade or otherwise, be lent, resold, hired out or otherwise circulated without the prior consent of the publisher in any form of binding or cover other than that in which it is published and without a similar condition including this condition being imposed on the subsequent purchaser.

First published in Great Britain 1988 by Mills & Boon Limited

© Annabel Murray 1988

Australian copyright 1988 Philippine copyright 1988 This edition 1988

ISBN 0 263 75980 6

Set in Times Roman 10 on 11¼ pt. 01-0588-57440 C

Printed and bound in Great Britain by Collins, Glasgow

For Enid,
my 'arty-crafty'
friend.

CHAPTER ONE

IT WAS the quiet end of a quiet day. The little seaside town lay somnolent beneath the August sun. No breath of air came to stir the dust motes suspended along the beams that penetrated the window and filled the shop with its oppressive heat.

Behind the counter, Briony Kent kicked off her flat, leather-thonged sandals and luxuriated in the coolness of the tiles beneath her feet. Nearly closing time. A sense of peace and contentment pervaded her whole being.

'Right! Where is he?'

The shop bell continued to vibrate with the violence of the tall man's entrance. Briony, interrupted in her task of adding up the day's takings, looked up with an abstracted frown to meet cold, grey eyes in a lean, angry face.

'Sorry?'

'Don't pretend not to understand!' His deep, gravelly voice vibrated around her. 'I'm not one to be deceived by large, innocent blue eyes and a pretty face. Where's Matthew?'

Slightly nonplussed, Briony stared into the strongly masculine face. It wasn't a handsome face, by any means, but it *was* an interesting one—dark and brooding. Unexpectedly, despite his abrasive manner, she felt a leap of physical response to his unquestionable attraction.

'Matthew Rawlinson?'

'Who else?' Impatience marred his cultured tones.

'He's not here.'

'You don't deny he comes here—regularly?'

'No, of course not. He...'

'When will he be back?' Though the counter was between them, Briony felt menaced by the tall stranger. He bore all the aspects of violence scarcely held in check: a nerve twitched in the lean cheek, his broad shoulders were tautly held, his hands clenched.

'I'm not sure. Tomorrow, maybe. Perhaps Wednesday.'

'Not tonight?' He sounded disbelieving.

'Not on a Monday. We don't...'

'Got another love nest for Mondays, has he?'

Briony slapped the account book down on the counter. She didn't have to put up with this.

'Look! I don't know who you are or what you want with Matthew. But I *do* know what you're insinuating and I...'

'And you're going to deny you're having an affair with Rawlinson!'

'I *do* deny it!' Briony said with an emphatic toss of her red curls. 'Though what it's got to do with you...'

'How much do you know about Rawlinson?' His voice lashed at her angrily.

'Not much. Matthew doesn't discuss his private life.'

'Hardly surprising.' The grey eyes were insolently assessing. 'I should imagine his mind's on other things. Such as five-foot nothing of blue-eyed redhead, with a waist my hands could span and a very kissable mouth, if your tastes run that way.' Something brooding in the atmosphere made it sound as though he found the prospect rather appealing himself, and Briony shifted uneasily, wishing she were not alone on the premises.

Beneath the anger, she sensed a virile charm which, she suspected, had breached the defences of more than one feminine citadel. She was suddenly conscious that, because of the warm August day, she wore very little beneath her Indian cotton dress. Consequently, it moulded closely to her small but full breasts, and clung sinuously around her slender legs. She strove for dignity, unaware how the faint air of aloofness increased her attraction.

'Look, Mr...?'

'Munro. Teale Munro.'

'Are you some kind of detective, Mr Munro?' He didn't look like her preconceived image of a private eye—seedy and furtive. Beneath the anger, his countenance was open and frank. He was too well dressed.

'If I were, I'd scarcely be approaching you so directly. Oh, don't worry, Miss Kent,' he added with a touch of weary irony, 'you won't be featuring in any explicit photographs or in the courts. Nobody wants any scandal. Me least of all.'

'How do you know my name?' she demanded.

'Other people besides detectives ask questions. The lady in the antiques shop next door was most helpful.'

She would be, Briony fumed. Especially if it seemed like a chance of casting aspersions on her neighbours' characters. Mrs Moss had never approved of Briony Kent and her partner. She claimed their proximity detracted from her own trade.

'Are you going to tell me when and where I can find Matthew?' Teale Munro's impatient voice broke across her thoughts.

'If I knew, I wouldn't tell you,' Briony retorted with spirit. 'How do I know you don't mean him any harm?'

'You don't,' the man said grimly. 'It would serve him right if I did break his neck for him. And now, if you don't mind, I'll just take a look around, to satisfy myself you're telling the truth.'

'But I *do* mind!' Courageously, Briony planted herself in front of him as he moved towards the door that connected the shop and living quarters. 'Unless you're a policeman with a search warrant, you've no right.'

For a moment, she thought he might thrust her aside. But then the shop bell rang again. This time, Briony was relieved to see the short, plump, sari-clad figure of her partner, carrying a large cardboard box filled to overflowing.

'OK,' Teale Munro said grimly. 'You win this time. But I'll be back. Tell Matthew Rawlinson that.'

As the door slammed behind him, Briony sank into a chair. Her legs were shaking too much to hold her up. With a sigh of relief, Promilla Kadri dumped the box she carried on the counter and raised an enquiring brow.

'What was all that about?' The large, liquid dark eyes and brown face were concerned. And, when Briony had enlightened her, she said, 'I did warn you something like this could happen one day.'

'Don't rub it in,' Briony said ruefully. But this time Promilla might be right, she thought. The arrival of the somewhat mysterious Matthew Rawlinson on their horizons did look like causing trouble.

He'd turned up one day in June. Predictably, it was raining outside. Useless rain, Briony called it. Not an honest-to-goodness, get-it-over-with downpour, but a fine, persistent drizzle that hung over land and sea and looked set in for the day. Not exactly a day to tempt window-shoppers, Briony would have thought. It was miserable. And the man looked miserable as he stood, shoulders hunched against the weather, with his face almost pressed to the window, looking in at the display. It was a nice display. Briony had only just arranged it that morning. But it scarcely warranted such intent study in such weather. His thin raincoat was already soaked. The turned-up collar framed a thin, pale, bearded face with large, melancholy eyes. Always soft-hearted, Briony felt sorry for him.

'He looks half drowned,' she said. 'And he doesn't look well. Shall I ask him in?'

'Why not?' Promilla Kadri smiled. 'You usually do. Though the last one took fright. He thought you were trying to sell him something. You and your lame dogs,' she continued a little anxiously as Briony moved purposefully to the door. 'I just know some day one of them will turn out to be trouble.'

'Would you like to shelter inside?' Briony asked the man. Even she was surprised by the alacrity of his response.

'May I? I was trying to make up my mind to come in and ask you something.' He was older than she'd thought from her first sight of him. Fortyish. He was well spoken, but there was a slight hesitancy in his speech, not quite a stutter; and a nerve twitched restlessly in one cheek. As he spoke, he peeled off his sodden raincoat, revealing shabby cords and a baggy T-shirt. His bare feet were encased in open-toed and very wet sandals.

'I'll put the kettle on,' Promilla said with a resigned sigh. Briony's lame dogs were never allowed to depart without refreshment of some kind. Most recipients of her goodwill were passing vagrants, but there was something slightly different about this one.

'You wanted to ask a question,' Briony reminded the man.

'Yes, if you're sure I'm not being a nuisance. You're not too busy?'

'Now, do we look busy?' Briony laughed as she indicated the empty shop. 'A wet Monday morning doesn't bring many customers our way. Sit down, won't you?'

Despite the chair she offered, the man seemed less interested in asking his question than in inspecting his surroundings. He surveyed the well stocked shelves and wall space with intent eyes that looked too large for his thin face. It would be even thinner, Briony thought, without the moustache and beard and frame of overlong hair.

'Are you keen on art?' she ventured after he had spent several minutes in silent contemplation before a large canvas—a seascape that embodied the colour and atmosphere of the Devonshire coastline.

'Mmmn,' he said non-committally. He moved on. 'Nice place you have here. Do you do much business?'

'Yes, in the holiday season we get a lot of passing trade. Even out of season, there's a fairly regular turnover. People buy their birthday and Christmas gifts from us. Then, of course, we travel to craft fairs all over the country. Sometimes further afield.'

Briony was faintly amused. He was dressed like everyone's idea of an impoverished artist. She suspected he was engaged in a form of market research—to find out what demand there might be locally for his own work, perhaps. She didn't remember having seen him before. Maybe he was new to the district. A lot of craft workers moved into tourist areas, hoping to make a business out of their talents. It wasn't that easy. Many had tried and failed. But he looked so pathetically vulnerable, she hadn't the heart to tell him that outright.

'We sell a lot of work on commission. Local artists and craftsmen bring us their finished products. If they're up to the standards we set for the shop, we display them for a month. Perhaps you have something you'd like us to sell for you?'

'No.'

Promilla came through from the back of the shop, carrying a tray. She handed round large mugs of coffee and generous slices of her own home-made cake. Briony decided it was time for introductions.

'I'm Briony—Briony Kent,' she offered. 'This is my friend and partner, Promilla Kadri.' She looked at him expectantly.

'Matthew,' he said. 'Matthew Rawlinson.' He continued to prowl as he drank his coffee, and munched on the cake as though he hadn't eaten for a week. He stopped before the canvas that had interested him earlier. 'How much would something like this fetch?'

'It's priced at five hundred pounds,' Briony told him.

'*That* much?' He was obviously impressed. He moved on, came to a flight of roped-off stairs. 'What's up there?'

'The studio,' Promilla told him. 'We don't just run a shop. We work up there when the shop's closed, and occasionally we take students. Evening classes. We have the occasional one in summer, but it's mostly through the winter months.'

'Students?' Suddenly the dark eyes were very much alert in the pale face. 'You mean, you teach people to paint?'

'Among other things. We also have a pottery out back,' Briony explained. 'We do fabric design as well. In fact, between us we cater for most forms of art and craft.'

Matthew Rawlinson returned yet again to the painting which seemed to exert a peculiar fascination over him.

'Could you teach *me* to paint like that?'

'Not exactly like that,' Briony protested, then at his downcast look, she added, 'I mean, there's no merit in acquiring someone else's style. If you have any talent, you could be taught to develop your own. Have you done any painting at all?'

'Some,' he admitted, 'but nothing like that.'

'Would you like to see the studio?' Briony asked. 'We have a permanent exhibition of paintings and craftwork up there. It isn't usually open on a Monday, but if you're interested . . .'

He nodded and was close on her heels as she unhooked the rope and led the way upstairs. The studio was vast. Consisting of several rooms knocked into one, it occupied a similar floorspace to the shop and living quarters below it. The air was heavy with the scent of paint and turps. More paintings hung on the walls. Several easels stood at one end of the room, holding paintings in various stages of execution. Matthew paid particular attention to these.

'And at this end,' Briony told him, 'Promilla takes her students for all kinds of fabric work, from the actual pattern design through to dressmaking, patchwork, collage, anything you care to mention.' But Matthew was interested only in the paintings.

'So you're the artist?'

'Artist, potter, sculptor.'

'Any of your own work here?'

'The picture you were looking at downstairs is one of mine.'

'I suppose you charge for lessons? How much?'

Briony looked at his shabby clothing, then into anxious brown eyes and halved her normal fee. A look of relief flooded his face.

'When can I start?'

'Tomorrow night?' Briony was touched by his eagerness. She knew Promilla was going to call her all kinds of a fool. But it wouldn't be the first time she'd lowered her rates. Besides, if Matthew Rawlinson had no talent he wouldn't last long. And if he *had* talent it would be criminal not to help him develop it.

Now, two months later, Matthew was still attending regularly, and Briony had no doubt of his talent and enthused daily to her friend. But Promilla, while admitting his work to be exceptional, expressed concern. The colours on his palette were harsh and unconventional. In his landscapes, vivid red skies predominated. There was a kind of frenzied desperation to his brush strokes that was reminiscent of Van Gogh at his most disturbed.

'There's something about him that worries me, Briony. I'm not sure what it is. But I'll tell you frankly, I don't like the idea of you being alone here with him when I'm away on buying trips.' Briony was so keen to help her new student that she allowed him to use the studio at will. She never knew quite when he would turn up. But he never came again on a Monday.

'He's just a bit eccentric,' Briony reassured her. 'A lot of artists are.' She laughed. 'I sometimes think I'm a bit eccentric myself!'

Now Promilla was looking at her friend with concern.

'That Munro man really got to you, didn't he? If we were the drinking kind, I'd prescribe a stiff whisky. As it is, I think I'd better put the kettle on.'

Briony picked up the heavy cardboard box and followed her through to the kitchen.

'I'm all right. I don't think I was in any danger except, perhaps, of losing my temper.' She hated conflict. 'Phew, this box is a weight! Did you have a good day?'

'Splendid. I'll let you have a gloat in a minute.' The two girls shared a taste for Victoriana and 1920s memorabilia, and Promilla had been to an auction sale in the next county. 'You can guess who was there, of course?'

'Mrs Moss from next door?'

'The same. She wasn't pleased when I walked off with some of the best pieces.'

'So she'll be feeling even more vindictive towards us.' Briony revealed the fact that Teale Munro had been making enquiries about them. 'She's probably hoping he knows something to discredit us, so we'll have to move.'

'Not a chance,' Promilla said cheerfully as she handed Briony a mug of tea. 'Our consciences are totally clear. The woman's unreasonable. It's not as if we *sell* antiques. And not everyone can afford to give antiques as gifts. If the silly woman looked at it sensibly, she'd realise we're of mutual benefit. And, with trade as it is, there's room for both of us in Gwinvercombe. I've never regretted moving here, have you?'

'Never,' Briony confirmed.

Her friendship with Promilla Kadri was of some ten years standing. Promilla was six years older than Briony. They'd met originally in London, when Briony had been an art student. They'd bumped into each other, literally, in an antiques shop in Camden Passage. During apologies and subsequent conversation they'd discovered many mutual interests and taken a liking to each other.

In those days, Promilla had worked for her parents, who ran an artists' supply shop in one of London's many side streets, but she was just branching out, selling her craftwork from a stall in Covent Garden.

Briony had sometimes envied the other girl's warm relationship with her parents. Briony had never felt particularly close to her widowed father. She supposed he was fond of her and she of him. But he'd already been middle-aged when she was born; and he always seemed preoccupied with farm business. He hadn't approved of her going to London to study art. He felt sure that London and all art students were thoroughly decadent, and the outcome of her student days had only confirmed him in his opinion; though, to do him justice, he had stood by her.

Over the intervening years, Briony had kept in touch with her friend. And then, two years ago, when Briony's personal life had touched rock bottom, Promilla, who was herself going through a bad patch, following the death of her parents, had been kind and understanding.

They had both felt in need of a new start, a change of scenery.

After much deliberation, they'd settled on the north Devonshire coast, and on Gwinvercombe in particular. Gwinvercombe overlooked Morte Bay, with Morte Point to the north and Baggy Point lining the southern side of the bay. Consisting of a single main street that dropped down to the waterfront car park, the little town had much to recommend it—not only as a setting for the commercial enterprise they planned, but also as a home. For despite its popularity with tourists, it remained relatively unspoiled.

The worst problem they encountered was that of the lanes leading into the little seaside town, which became choked with cars whose drivers either would not or could not reverse. Those residents more interested in self-seeking commercialism than aesthetics suggested the lanes should be widened. But in Briony and Promilla's opinion that would worsen the situation, opening the way for coachloads of the rowdier element. Besides, traffic-choked or not, the winding lanes were part of the character of the place.

The countryside overlooking the bay had a subtle serenity. From the upstairs studio windows the two girls could see the bay, with its wide gleaming water, boats and trailing reflections. And in rough weather they could both see and hear the white breakers as they leapt and staggered and fell with the roar and clangour of grinding pebbles.

'No, I've never regretted coming here,' Briony repeated.

'It's just about closing time,' Promilla said. 'I'll lock up and you can unwrap the goodies.'

Beyond the kitchen was the spacious living-room shared by the two girls. Visitors agreed that entering their apartment was like crossing a frontier. The High Street

building was an old one, with large rooms and pro-
portionately lofty ceilings, and the living-room was
crammed with Victoriana, as well as the Eastern trea-
sures which had belonged to Promilla's parents. Lining
the terracotta walls were Oriental naïve paintings and
Chinese household gods. Sepia photos flanked religious
statues from several cultures. Glass cases of wax flowers
and pink seashells stood cheek by jowl with leering
Indian masks. Promilla had also brought her late parents'
rich hoard of oriental furniture and rugs.

Carefully, Briony removed the paper from her friend's
latest purchases.

'Like them?' Promilla called from the kitchen, from
which came the fragrant smell of a curry prepared earlier
and now being warmed through.

'Like them? I love them! No wonder Mrs Moss was
furious.' The major find, so far as she was concerned,
was the enormous traditional patchwork quilt in subtle
colours. 'I've always wanted one of these on my bed.'

Her enthusiasm had temporarily banished the twin
problems of Matthew Rawlinson and Teale Munro from
her mind. But as they sat down to eat she found herself
thinking about the aggressive stranger.

'I wonder if he *will* come back?'

'You sound almost as if you hope he will.' Promilla
eyed her friend curiously.

'No, not exactly,' Briony demurred. 'But I *am* curious
as to why he wanted to see Matthew.'

'Why not ask Matthew?' Promilla suggested.

'Matthew! Elevenses!'

Matthew had been crouched over the easel since eight-
thirty that morning. Now, as Briony entered the studio,
carrying two mugs of coffee, he sat up, stretched his
cramped body and looked eagerly at her for her opinion.

'What do you think?'

She took a sip of her coffee before giving his work her critical consideration. At last, she sighed wonderingly.

'It's terrific, Matthew, as always. I just can't fault it.'

Despite this unstinted praise, he seemed dissatisfied. By now, Briony had realised that Matthew suffered from the most tremendous inferiority complex.

'It *can't* be that good. There must be something wrong with it. You're just being kind. I'll never paint like you.' He got up and prowled restlessly around the studio, his eyes devouring the works in various stages of completion. Some were awaiting a coat of varnish. Others were not yet framed. And on an easel was a rough outline of Briony's next composition. 'I just can't get it right.' Matthew shook his shaggy head in frustration.

'Matt! I've told you before. You don't *need* to paint like me. You have your own style.' Briony's paintings reflected her nature, warm yet serene. She had evolved a technique of glazing pictures with wax for a deep matt finish that added to their enigmatic appeal, which had been much praised after her last submission to the Royal Academy. 'I'd like to take some of your work up to London,' she told Matthew, 'to a gallery I know.' But Matthew was shaking his head. She'd said this to him before and, as always, he became agitated.

'No, not yet. I'm not ready. I may *never* be ready!'

Sometimes, Briony wondered if Promilla was right and there *was* some instability in Matthew's character.

'You never did tell me where and when you first started painting,' she reminded him.

'No, I didn't.' He said it with an air of finality, and she knew he was in one of his uncommunicative moods. His coffee was only half finished, but he bent once more over his easel, already eager to be back at his composition.

Briony had been waiting for the right moment to ask him about Teale Munro. She was a little afraid of the effect on him if she told him the other man was looking for him. It would be a tragedy if Matthew stopped coming to the studio. But now she knew it would be useless to mention yesterday's visitor. Matthew had deliberately switched off. He wouldn't hear a word.

The noise of a buzzer being sounded furiously told her the shop was getting busy and Promilla needed help.

'Staying to lunch today, Matthew?' she asked as she gathered up their mugs. Some days, he refused almost ungraciously. He had a prickly pride. Occasionally, it allowed him to accept the girls' hospitality. More often, it didn't. Today, however, he nodded assent without taking his eyes from the work before him.

'Do you think you'll be able to hold the fort during the lunch hour?' Promilla asked Briony during a temporary lull in serving.

'I should think so. I'll leave the communicating door open so I can hear the bell. Are you lunching out?'

'If I'm lucky. I had a telephone call while you were upstairs. I've got to take that order over to Ilfracombe. "Lady" Wareing wants delivery yesterday—as usual. Sometimes she deigns to offer me lunch.'

Promilla had a regular demand from a shop in Ilfracombe for the strikingly original cushions and quilts she designed and made. Sukie Wareing's 'title' was an ironic one bestowed because of her autocratic manner.

'It's good of you girls to put up with my fads,' Matthew said as he sat at the kitchen table. Once in a while, he remembered his manners sufficiently to thank them.

'I've often thought of becoming a vegetarian myself,' Briony said as she set a tastefully arranged salad in front of him. 'I know all the health and conscience arguments for it,' she went on half apologetically, 'but I'm afraid I enjoy meat too much to give it up altogether.'

Matthew shrugged. 'I used to be into organic vegetable gardening before...' He stopped abruptly. 'Now I can't be bothered. There isn't time. There's never enough time.' He began to bolt his food, and Briony knew he was eager to return to the studio.

'I've never asked you, Matthew—do you live locally?' She knew immediately that the question had been a mistake, as a hunted expression crossed his face. She wouldn't get a straight answer and she could see the relief in his eyes as the sound of the shop bell made a reply unnecessary.

'Be with you in a minute,' she called to an invisible customer. She put a fresh fruit salad in front of Matthew, leaning over him as she did so to collect his empty plate.

'What a cosy domestic scene!'

Briony started and nearly dropped the plate. Indignantly, she turned round to see who had dared to violate the privacy of the living quarters behind the shop. But really she knew there was no need to look; she had recognised that throaty voice.

'Mr Munro...' she began. But she was interrupted by Matthew, who lurched to his feet, his face contorted with fury. It was difficult, looking from one to the other, to decide which of the two men looked angrier.

'Munro! What are *you* doing here?'

'I might ask you the same.' Teale Munro's voice was harsh, contemptuous. 'Except that I don't need to ask. Up to your old tricks again, are you, Matthew?'

'How did you know...?' Matthew began.

'You were seen. By a mutual acquaintance, who lost no time in telling Rhoda.'

'And Rhoda *had* to tell *you*, of course!' Matthew sounded defeated now. It was as if his anger had drained from him, leaving him bowed and limp.

'Which entailed telephoning me in London, in the middle of a very important conference, and dragging me down here.' The dagger-sharp glare of grey eyes encompassed Briony, too, taking in her long floral skirt, the skimpy T-shirt, the loops of amber beads about her slender neck. 'You always did have a penchant for redheads, didn't you, Matthew? I see this time you've found one who shares your bizarre tastes.' At the contempt in his tone, Briony stiffened. What did he mean by that? She was soon enlightened as Teale went on, 'Isn't it about time you grew up, Matthew? There's something extremely ridiculous and pathetic about ageing hippies.'

'Was that insult aimed at me, too?' Briony asked quietly—deceptively quietly. Those who knew her well could have told Teale that when she was most quiet she was most angry. Her face, haloed by its wealth of fiery-red curls, had paled, making the dusting of freckles across her nose stand out more noticeably. Her blue eyes held storm clouds. His shrug further incensed her.

'If the cap fits, as they say!'

'Mr Munro, you're trespassing,' she pointed out. 'This is my home, not a public thoroughfare. If you have anything to say to Mr Rawlinson, please say it elsewhere.'

'*Mr Rawlinson,*' he mocked. 'Very formal all of a sudden, aren't you? Is that meant to convince me there's nothing going on between you two? Because, if so, let me tell you it's a failure, like *Mr Rawlinson* himself.'

Briony looked at Matthew, expecting him to flare up in his own defence. But, tall though he was, and better-nourished than when the girls had first met him—principally due to their efforts—he seemed to have shrunk in upon himself.

'Are you going to stand there,' Briony demanded, 'and let this man insult you?'

'He's done nothing else for the last eighteen years,' Matthew muttered. 'And he's right—I *am* a failure. I told *you* that. I'll never be anything else.'

'If you take that attitude and allow yourself to be browbeaten, of course you won't,' Briony retorted. She turned on Teale Munro, far angrier on Matthew's behalf than on her own. 'What right have you to belittle Matthew? How can you deliberately set out to undermine another person's confidence? It's cruel and arrogant. What makes *you* a better man, fit to judge *him*? He...' Her voice caught on a sob, not of anger now, but of compassion for Matthew's broken, defeated stance.

'How very touching!' Teale Munro said scornfully. 'How *do* you do it, Matthew? First Rhoda, then Charlene, and now Miss Briony Kent, RA. What sort of man lets himself be bolstered up and supported by women?'

'*You* wouldn't understand.' Matthew said it wearily. He brushed past Teale Munro, into the shop, and headed for the outer door.

'Matthew,' Briony called after him anxiously, 'where are you going? What about...?' She was going to say 'your painting', but he forestalled her.

'I'm not in the mood now, Briony. Perhaps I never will be again. Sorry, and thanks.' The door jangled and closed.

'Sorry about that, *Briony*!' Teale Munro's hatefully mocking voice came from close behind her, making her start away nervously. 'But it would seem Matthew's "not in the mood" for *you*, now I've reminded him of too many things he'd rather forget.'

Briony's face turned from white to red. Teale Munro obviously thought he'd interrupted an assignation, that his arrival had deterred Matthew from making love to her!

In that moment, she wished she had never met either man. For the last two years, here in Gwinvercombe, her life had been peaceful, free of the conflict she disliked so much. But, though she hated arguments and rows, Briony had a fiery temper. She deplored it and most of the time she was able to control it. Now she bit on her lip and counted to ten. She was tempted to take Teale Munro up to the studio and show him just why Matthew came here. But she didn't know what Matthew's re-action would be. He might be furious, especially if he'd told no one about his painting. The odds were that he hadn't. It would be on a par with his almost abnormal secretiveness.

'Please go, Mr Munro,' she said stiffly. 'You've achieved your object. You've "rescued" Matthew from my clutches. Be satisfied.'

'Oh, I'm far from satisfied,' he told her somewhat ambiguously, his voice a deep drawl.

'What more could you possibly want?' Now they were alone, she was aware once more of his swarthy attrac-tiveness. On his first visit, he had worn a suit that screamed Savile Row. Today, he wore faded hip-hugging jeans—designer jeans, admittedly—and a silver-grey sweatshirt that matched his eyes. But despite the casual clothes he was immaculately groomed, from crow-black hair to well kept fingernails and polished shoes.

'The answers to a lot of questions.' Teal Munro was not unaware of her appraisal, and he let his eyes roam over her in a blatant scrutiny of her flushed, heart-shaped face and, more particularly, her figure, noting her un-studied sexuality.

'I doubt if I have anything of interest to tell you.' Briony assumed he meant to question her about Matthew. Before he spoke, his mouth widened into a one-sided smile that seemed to mock himself rather than her, and she knew that she'd misunderstood.

'Oh, I disagree, Miss Briony Kent. Under different circumstances, I think I might find you very interesting indeed!'

CHAPTER TWO

EVEN in the face of this provoking remark, Briony did not sacrifice her natural dignity. She drew herself up to her full five feet two inches. Only the widely spaced, sapphire-blue eyes betrayed the intensity of her feelings.

'Mr Munro, I dislike having to be rude to people. So I'm asking you once more, politely, to go.'

'Oh, I'm going, Miss Kent.' Despite the sarcastic note, his laughter had a vital sound that, under other circumstances, Briony would have found very attractive. 'But only because I want a word with our mutual friend Rawlinson, before he disappears under his stone again. I'll be back.'

Tensely, she watched him go. She was angry. But she was a woman, and capable of appreciating Teale Munro's height, his deceptively lean build. There was power in the wide shoulders, arrogance in the set of his dark head. She knew nothing about him, yet she suspected him of being a man who had made his mark in life. His whole carriage, his long, easy stride, bore the unmistakable stamp of success and self-confidence. Which made it all the more despicable, she reminded herself, that he should taunt Matthew with *his* failures.

'It's a good job I don't work in a china shop,' Briony muttered to herself as the door closed behind him and his departing steps continued to echo in her mind, 'because I feel like smashing something.' Though her past relationships with the opposite sex had not always been very happy ones, she couldn't remember ever feeling *this* furious with a man.

Her nerves remained distinctly on edge for the next hour or so, until Promilla returned and Briony could let off steam to her friend.

'Has it occurred to you,' Promilla asked diffidently, 'that Mr Munro might have good reason for the things he said to Matthew? Matthew *is* a bit of a mystery man.'

'So is Teale Munro,' Briony argued. 'We've known Matthew for a couple of months now. He's never been any trouble. He's a darned good artist. And I like him. We know absolutely nothing about Teale Munro. Anyway,' she concluded with a toss of her red curls, 'I'm going to try and forget about the wretched man. I don't expect he *will* come back again, not now he's tracked Matthew down. The trouble is, Matthew may not come back, either. It'll be a crime,' she said fiercely, 'if that man's managed to put him off! Matthew could have had a great future before him.'

Despite her declaration that she intended to forget Teale Munro, it was surprising how often her thoughts returned to him during the evening that followed. When she wasn't painting, which she did very quickly and intensively, in bursts of almost manic energy, Briony normally had a talent for total relaxation. She loved to read, or watch old films or play with the cats. Tonight, neither her book—a shudder-a-minute horror—nor an old black and white 'weepy' on television could hold her interest. Not even the presence of her favourite cat, Tara, on her knee could soothe her.

'How dare he refer to me as an ageing hippy?' she demanded of Promilla, unconsciously stroking the Siamese's honey-coloured fur the wrong way. 'I don't deliberately create *any* image. I just wear what I like.' It was true. Briony could as easily have been wearing one of the old twenties costumes in her collection. She loved dressing up, even to serve in the shop, and most customers enjoyed seeing her individual clothes, they were appreciative and admiring. The Siamese took exception to her mood and jumped down to curl on the hearthrug beside a silver tabby.

Promilla's head was bent over the new design she was working on, of fat quilted pansies on a silver background.

'Mr Munro certainly seems to have made an impression on you.' She looked up speculatively at Briony. 'I only had a brief glimpse of him, but he looked rather dishy. Didn't *you* think he was handsome?'

'Not handsome, exactly,' Briony said consideringly, unaware of her friend's amused smile. 'I'd call it an interesting face. Intelligent.' Then, indignantly, 'Anyway, handsome is as handsome does, and his appearance is of no concern to me.'

Strange, though, how in bed that night, even with her eyes closed, she could clearly see Teale Munro's dark, lively face with its irregular features, the piercing grey eyes, cold in anger. His nose, she'd noted, had been broken at some time, and she wondered how it had happened. Somehow it did not mar his appearance, but added rather to its interest. She could even recall exactly how the thick, dark hair lay at the nape of his strong neck. Irritated by this persistent image, Briony flicked on the light and tried to banish it by reading, until finally she fell asleep with the book still clutched in her hand.

'Four or five letters for you this morning,' Promilla was sorting through the post when Briony emerged from her room, yawning and heavy-eyed. 'One from France. Iseult, I expect? And one for me from my great-aunt in Karachi.'

'Is she still pressing you to go and visit her?' Briony flicked through her own mail. Two orders, two cheques in payment for some paintings she'd sold during a recent exhibition in London and the letter from Iseult. This treat she put on one side to read later.

'Yes. Since my grandparents died, she's my only living relative back there. I suppose I ought to go one of these days, while she's still alive.' Promilla had never visited her parents' country of origin. 'Aren't you going to read your letter?'

'Not yet. Have you seen the time? We're neither of us washed and dressed yet, and Wednesday's market day. Gwinvercombe will be humming.'

'True, and we need to do some food shopping. One of us had better pop out when there's an opportunity.'

It was Briony who eventually slipped away, while Promilla was dealing with a regular customer for her wares.

The August day was hot but invigorating, hazy without the glare. The pavements thronged with dawdling holiday-makers. Briony, making the most of her legitimate freedom, strolled down the narrow street towards the market stalls ranged alongside the car park. She sniffed appreciatively at the ozone-scented air. The sea was peaceful today, glittering silver beneath a clear blue sky, the surf subsiding on stones with a gentle surge, slap and a sigh.

She recognised one or two residents mingling with the tourists, and enjoyed a few moments' repartee with some of the regular stallholders. Briony and Promilla were, in general, popular with the Devonshire people. Only their neighbour, Mrs Moss, continued to resent them.

Buying vegetables made her think of Matthew. He hadn't turned up at the studio this morning and she felt a renewed spurt of anger against Teale Munro which threatened to spoil the idyllic summer day. But she was only annoyed on Matthew's behalf, she reminded herself firmly. She couldn't care less about Teale Munro, or his opinion of her.

With a heavily laden basket on her arm, she toiled back up the hill. But fatigue was forgotten and she hastened her steps as she saw a familiar figure hesitating outside the shop.

'Matthew!' she panted. 'I'm so glad to see you. I thought you weren't coming any more.'

He turned to look at her, his eyes dull in his pale face.

'I nearly didn't. I wasn't planning to go in——' he nodded his head at the doorway '—but somehow I found myself walking this way.'

'Why on earth shouldn't you go in?' Briony set her basket down and put her hand on his arm.

'I didn't think you'd want me here any more after all that trouble yesterday.'

'Matthew,' she said firmly, 'if you want to come here and paint, that's OK by me. You know how I feel about your work. I'd have been very disappointed in you if you *hadn't* come back.'

His expression lightened and he made no further demur as she opened the door and ushered him in. In fact, once inside, he lost no time in mounting the stairs to the studio.

'Did you ask him for an explanation?' Promilla followed her friend through to the kitchen where she was unloading her purchases.

'No.'

'Don't you think you should?'

Briony paused in her task and looked at her partner.

'Obviously *you* think I should. I can ask him, but he may clam up on me as usual.'

'I think we're entitled to know just what kind of trouble Matthew is in. Besides,' a glimmer of a smile lit Promilla's round face, 'you know you're dying to find out more about Teale Munro.'

'I'm not!' Briony denied.

'Briony, you haven't shown that much reaction to a man in two or three years. Maybe you're coming back to life again?'

'If I ever let any man get in my hair again, it certainly won't be Teale Munro,' Briony retorted, but when she re-entered the shop she headed for the upstairs studio.

'Need any help?' she asked as her excuse. It was a long time since they'd pretended Matthew came here for formal lessons. There was nothing more she could teach him. She didn't even charge him for the use of the studio. Then when he merely grunted a negative, she went on 'Matthew, I'm not prying, but *who is* Teale Munro? What does he want?'

With reluctance, Matthew tore his gaze away from his painting.

'He's my brother-in-law.'

'Oh!' Whatever Briony had expected, it hadn't been that.

'He's never had much time for me,' Matthew said. 'But you gathered that. He only bothers with me because Rhoda does.' And that was the most she was going to get out of Matthew, Briony realised as he took up his palette once more.

'So Teale Munro was only sorting out his wife's brother?' Promilla was relieved. 'Just a domestic spat. Nothing criminal.'

'No, nothing criminal,' but Briony said it almost wearily. She should be relieved, too, but she felt unaccountably depressed.

'It's always disappointing,' Promilla said to nobody in particular, 'when you find an attractive man's already spoken for.'

'Is that what you think?' Briony laughed with unconvincing incredulity. 'I just feel sorry for any woman married to Teale Munro. I wonder what sort of inferiority complex he gives *her*?'

* * *

'But you *know* now why Matthew comes here!' Across the counter, Briony faced the angry man who had erupted into the shop that Friday morning. Why did he always choose a moment when she was alone? She could have done with Promilla's moral support. But her friend was out on a delivery.

'I *think* I know why he comes here,' Teale Munro corrected her. His lean countenance was taut and austere. 'And I thought the fact that I'd caught him at it would be sufficient deterrent. It seems I was wrong. Either he's developed a more determined nature than I gave him credit for, or you have a more potent effect on him than I suspected.' His eyes raked her from head to toe, unwilling appreciation of her appearance in their grey depths.

'Mr Munro, I've already told you, twice, that I'm not having an affair with your brother-in-law. I had hoped you'd taken my word for it. And after you'd spoken to Matthew on Tuesday...'

'Miss Kent, I would *like* to believe you, perhaps more than you imagine. But when I spoke to Matthew he told me absolutely nothing! Matthew Rawlinson can be a slippery, close-mouthed bastard when he likes.'

Briony had to agree with the sentiment, though she wouldn't have put it in those words. And she was a little annoyed with Matthew herself now. He and his brother-in-law might not hit it off, but that was no reason why he shouldn't exonerate her from Teale Munro's unpleasant suspicions. She didn't want gratitude for all the help she'd given him, but she wouldn't have minded that much consideration. She came to a reluctant decision.

'I think you'd better come upstairs with me, Mr Munro.'

'Why? Isn't Matthew around today? Sorry, but I've never fancied sharing his mistresses.'

Afterwards, Briony wondered what had got into her. She'd never believed before that people actually saw red when they got mad. But maybe it was just the colour of his sweatshirt, against which she was pounding small, clenched fists. She had flown at him, dashed around the counter and launched her attack without any thought for the consequences.

Taken by surprise, it was a second or two before he succeeded in restraining her flailing hands. The sensation of his fingers clasped around her wrists firmly but not hurtfully, his closeness, made her shiver.

'Why, you little hell-cat!' There was a strange note in his voice that could have been mistaken for admiration as he looked down into her set, angry face.

Briony's rage evaporated as quickly as it had come. She was trembling violently—with the aftermath of her sudden passion, she told herself.

'Let go of me!' she demanded.

'With pleasure.' He released her, but her flesh still scorched where he had held her. 'But it was *you* who threw yourself into my arms,' he reminded her. Strangely, he wasn't sneering at her now. The words were not insulting as the others had been. Instead, he was smiling. The one-sided, crooked grimace lit up his face to a startling degree, accentuating the impact of his male attraction.

'When I said upstairs,' Briony told him through teeth that were clenched to stop them chattering, 'I meant to the studio. Over there.' She nodded towards the flight of open-tread stairs. 'If you want to know why Matthew comes here, I'll show you.' She went ahead, taking care not to brush against him in passing. But she wished she had let him precede her when she remembered that the skirt she wore today was a skimpy one, and that the angle of the stairs gave him an unrestricted view of her slender, shapely legs. She was inordinately glad to reach the studio door.

'Matthew, you've got a visitor.' And, at the look on the painter's face, she added, 'I'm sorry, but, if it's the only way to stop Mr Munro making his unfounded allegations, he's got to know what you're doing here.' A little reproachfully, she continued, 'You should have told him yourself. It would have saved a lot of trouble.'

At first sight of Teale Munro, Matthew had made an instinctive move to hide his work. But he seemed to realise the impossibility of doing so and, with a gesture of resignation, he got up and walked to the far end of the studio. Briony watched him anxiously. Matthew was such a sensitive plant.

'Rawlinson painted this?' There was a note of incredulity in Teale Munro's voice and Briony glanced sharply at him, unsure whether it was praise or censure.

'And this one, and this one.' She led him around the large room. He might as well know the whole of it.

There was a long, tense silence as Teale moved from painting to painting and back again. He knew something about art, Briony guessed from the way he conducted his appraisal. At last he looked up, first at Matthew's uncompromisingly turned back and then at Briony's expectant heart-shaped face.

'He seems to have a strong predilection for red, especially red skies,' was his initial comment. Then, 'What do *you* think of his work?' he asked abruptly. 'You're the Royal Academician.'

'I think it's excellent,' she told him quietly. 'And I keep telling him so. But Matthew finds it hard to accept my opinion. And I can see why now: a man who is constantly being knocked down is bound to have a feeling of inferiority.'

A faint colour ran up Teale's tanned face, but he made no immediate reply. Instead, he returned to the paintings.

'Which was done first?' And, as she showed him, he asked, 'And the next?' And so on, until he came back to the current work.

'The progression is amazing, isn't it?' she asked him, unable to contain her eager enthusiasm. Wide, bright eyes fringed with thick, dark lashes looked frankly into his. For a moment, she had forgotten her resentment of him in their shared moment of appreciation.

'Amazing,' he agreed, but only he knew he referred to something else besides the painting. 'So, what next?'

'I'd like a London expert to see his work, but Matthew won't hear of it.'

'Same old Matthew,' Teale said obscurely. He looked down at Briony from his considerable height. 'It seems I owe you an apology, Miss Kent.' But then his tone changed to one of outright mischief. 'In view of all this industry, I agree it would seem Matthew hasn't had much time or energy for any other pursuits.'

For a moment, she stared at him uncomprehendingly. Then, she exploded, 'If that's your idea of an apology...'

'It isn't!' At once, he was suitably grave, the grey eyes serious. 'I have your word that there's nothing between you and Matthew—nothing at all?' He was actually waiting for an answer, she realised incredulously—and after all her assurances!

'You've had my word on that—twice already. Nothing has changed.'

'No? Except perhaps my respect and admiration for you,' he conceded. He held out a long lean hand. 'I apologise, Miss Kent, most humbly and sincerely. Can we shake on it?'

Briony felt an odd reluctance to put her hand into his, but when she had she felt as reluctant to withdraw it. His long fingers were pleasantly warm and dry, and his touch gave her an odd feeling of breathlessness. As she met his gaze, something about his expression was intensely disturbing, and her voice was a little unsteady as she accepted his apology.

'And you'll leave Matthew in peace now, to go on with his painting?' she asked to cover the momentary confusion she felt.

'On one condition. That he himself puts Rhoda's mind at rest. I won't have her worried and upset.' The concern in his voice reminded Briony that Teale Munro was a married man and she quickly withdrew her hand, which unaccountably still lingered in his.

'I'll talk to Matthew,' she promised.

'No need!' The harsh voice came from the other end of the studio, totally unlike Matthew's normally quiet, diffident tones. Incredibly, she'd forgotten he was there. 'I do have the use of my hearing, you know, when you've finished discussing me. And I'm not half-witted, either. I'll go up and see her today.' He strode towards the stairs.

'You *will* be back, Matthew?' Briony asked anxiously, before he could disappear.

'Yes.' His voice was still firm. 'For the first time in my life I've discovered something worth while. I'm not going to let go of that.'

'He means his painting,' Briony said hastily as she saw what seemed to be the return of doubt on Teale's hawklike features.

'Yes, of course,' he muttered abstractly. 'Well, I suppose I'd better go. I've trespassed enough on your time today.' Yet he made no move to go. 'May I come to see you again some time, on a different footing?' His deep voice was unusually husky. 'I'd like to...to make reparation for my behaviour.'

Briony felt a strange thrill of sensation run through her, even though she knew he only meant that any future visit to the shop would be on a civil, friendly basis. But he had no real reason for coming here. He didn't strike her as the arty-crafty type. And she could admit to

COLOUR THE SKY RED 37

herself, now he was no longer the villain of the piece,
that she found him too attractive for her peace of mind.
And he was married.

'I don't think there's much point,' she said, careful
to keep her voice level and matter of fact.

'I see.' Teale sounded unreasonably disappointed,
more so than the circumstances warranted. 'I suppose
I've blotted my copy-book too irrevocably. Ah, well!
Perhaps it's for the best.' He gave her a half-salute and
turned on his heel.

The next day was Saturday. Matthew didn't use the
studio at weekends. Briony suspected he would have done
if invited to do so. But, not unreasonably, Promilla had
suggested they were entitled to have the place to themselves. The shop was open on Saturday, of course. But
on Sunday they liked to catch up on their own work.
On this particular Sunday, a long silence reigned in the
studio. The normally talkative Briony was engrossed in
her thoughts.

'I'm seriously thinking of taking on an assistant to do
some of the making up,' Promilla said at last. She was
plying her needle while Briony painted. Briony was
working on a portrait of Promilla, something she'd
wanted to do for a long time. 'The demand is exceeding
my output,' Promilla went on.

'Hmm?' Briony said vaguely.

Promilla repeated her remark.

'Why not?' Briony agreed. 'The business can easily
stand another wage.'

'We shan't be seeing Mr Munro any more, then?'

'No.' Then, her attention fully secured, Briony looked
at her friend in surprise. 'But what's that got to do with
anything?' she demanded.

'Not much,' Promilla admitted. 'Except that you've obviously been elsewhere all afternoon. You're not usually so quiet when you're painting.'

'That doesn't mean I'm thinking about Teale Munro,' Briony said mendaciously. 'I could be thinking about anyone. Iseult, for instance.'

'Yes, that reminds me. What did she have to say in her letter?'

'Not much. But she didn't sound any happier than in the last one.'

'D'you think Jean-Luc *is* playing up?'

'Very likely. Iseult's pretty shrewd. If you don't mind, Prom, I think I'll write and invite her over for an extra visit. I know she doesn't normally come this time of year, but... Well, I've been a bit worried about her lately, and...'

'Of course I don't mind. You know I always like to see her.'

Matthew arrived mid-morning on the following Tuesday, as usual, and would have gone straight to work if Promilla hadn't urged Briony to intercept him.

'You'd better find out if he's done what his brother-in-law wanted.'

'Matthew!' Briony duly called, and he paused, one foot already on the bottom stair. 'Did you see your sister on Friday?'

'My sister?' He sounded puzzled rather than evasive.

'Rhoda, isn't it?'

'Rhoda's my wife, not my sister. And yes, I did see her!'

Briony was too speechless to detain and question him further, and he made good his opportunity to escape. Still looking slightly dazed, she went through into the kitchen where Promilla was making coffee. Ever frank, her partner spoke her mind.

'You look as if someone just pole-axed you. More trouble with Matthew?'

'No.' Briony sat down at the kitchen table. She felt strangely weak. She looked at her friend. 'He's *not* married, Prom.'

'Matthew isn't?'

'No, Teale isn't. Rhoda is *Matthew's* wife.'

'Ah, I see!' The words were heavily loaded, but Briony didn't take exception. She was reliving the moment when she'd learned Rhoda wasn't *Teale's* wife, remembering that unnerving spurt of something that had felt suspiciously like joy. 'Here's your coffee,' Promilla said. 'You look as if you need it. What did Matthew say exactly?' And, when Briony had told her, 'That only means Teale isn't married to *Rhoda*,' she pointed out. 'It doesn't mean he isn't married to someone else. Look before you leap, Briony.'

'I wasn't about to "leap" anywhere! I just wish I'd known before, that's all.' But, at her friend's words, Briony's heart had sunk abysmally.

'So that you wouldn't have been so discouraging when he asked if he could call round again?' The two girls had no secrets from each other.

'I suppose so.' Briony was prepared to admit that much.

'If by any chance he *is* single and he's really interested in you, that won't put him off. But find out a bit more about him before you go losing your heart.'

'I'm not likely to do that,' Briony argued. 'I'm not even sure I like him. It's just that there's something about him that makes me...Oh, I don't know.' She shivered.

'Chemistry,' Promilla said briskly. 'A dangerous ingredient in many relationships, as *you* very well know. *I* wouldn't fall in love with a man just because I found him physically attractive.'

'Nor would I—not these days,' Briony maintained. 'Do you ever wish,' she asked curiously, 'that your parents had "arranged" a marriage for you, in the old way?'

'Yes, sometimes. I would have liked to marry and have children. But I was brought up in England. I'm not sure I could reconcile the two cultures. I enjoy the freedom women in this country have.'

Every time the doorbell jangled that day, Briony looked up, heart in mouth, half expecting to see Teale Munro. But she knew it was an unreasonable expectation. He'd seemed to accept his *congé*.

Over lunch, Promilla put to an unusually talkative Matthew the questions Briony longed but feared to ask.

'What exactly is Teale Munro's connection with Rhoda?'

'She's his sister.' Matthew seemed surprised she even had to ask. 'His twin sister,' he qualified. 'They've always been very close. Hence the protective attitude.'

'Is Teale married?'

'No!' Matthew said the word explosively. The question seemed to annoy him, for as he replied he rose and pushed back his chair with a harsh, scraping noise. 'Thanks for the lunch. I'll get back to work now.' For some reason, he had withdrawn into his old, uncommunicative shell.

'*Now* what?' Promilla looked at Briony.

'Search me!'

When finally Teale Munro did come, Briony was out. She'd offered to deliver Promilla's latest batch of cushions and quilts to Sukie Wareing in Ilfracombe. Promilla didn't really enjoy driving. But it wasn't that. Briony felt that she just couldn't spend another day in the shop, in the state of nervous anticipation that had engulfed her all week. Teale Munro wasn't coming back and that was that. The best thing she could do was forget him and get on with her work and her life.

Briony drove fast, but with skill and verve. She loved cars, and the open sports model handled well. Unlike many people, she found driving relaxed her and she was in a sunny mood when she breezed back into the shop with a cheque for Promilla and another 'urgent' order.

'That settles it.' Promilla said. 'I'll have to advertise for an assistant.'

'Are you likely to find anyone with the right skills around here?'

'I can but try. Oh, by the way,' as Briony made for the stairs, 'your boyfriend's been in.'

Briony stood very still, one foot on the stairs, her back to her friend. She felt as if every hair on the nape of her neck had risen, and she knew her face had flushed betrayingly.

'Teale was here?'

Promilla giggled. 'I'm glad you don't pretend not to know who I mean.'

'Did he come to see Matthew?' Briony wouldn't let herself hope.

'He looked in on him, but he came to see you, as you very well know.'

'And I wasn't here,' Briony groaned. She turned back into the shop and saw her friend's round face creased into a beaming smile. 'What are you grinning at?' she enquired indignantly. 'It isn't funny.'

'You. You look so tragic. But there's no need—he's coming back.'

'He is? When? Oh, I look a mess! I'm all hot and windblown.'

'Don't panic. Relax. You've got plenty of time. He's coming at seven-thirty to take you out to dinner. A peace offering, he said!'

'Dinner? But I haven't said I'll ... How does he ...?'

'I told him I was sure you'd be happy to accept.'

'Prom! You didn't!' Briony was horrified. 'What *will* he think? He'll guess we've been discussing him.'

'It won't hurt him to have his ego repaired a little. He came in here looking more like a man going to the scaffold than a prospective lover. I don't think he was expecting a very warm reception.'

'Prom!' Briony expostulated again. 'You mustn't *say* things like that. He's *not* a prospective lover. It's probably just a guilt thing. You know, a way of apologising for his suspicions.'

'I don't believe that—any more than you *want* to believe it,' her friend told her.

When the doorbell rang that evening, promptly at seven-thirty, Briony felt her insides shake, and she experienced a fluttering weakness in her legs.

'Aren't you going to answer it?' Promilla asked.

'I can't!' Briony gasped. 'You go.'

As an amused Promilla moved to comply, Briony fled back into her bedroom and, for the tenth time since she'd dressed, she anxiously inspected her appearance. She hadn't been at all influenced by Teale's remark the other day about hippies, she told herself. But, all the same, she was conventionally dressed tonight.

She'd had the dress for years, but the silky navy material with its pattern of tiny white polka dots was cut in a style that did not date and she knew it suited her. Its colour deepened and intensified the blue of her eyes, made a foil for the rich red of her hair. Her flawless skin required very little make-up, other than a moisturiser. Her warm red mouth owed nothing to artifice.

The sound of voices in the outer room told her she could delay no longer and, with one last despairing glance at herself, she took a deep gulp of air and went out to face Teale Munro.

He very nearly took her breath away. She'd been a little afraid he might be in evening dress. Instead, he wore a charcoal-grey suit that had obviously been tailored to fit his tall, lithe body. A gleaming white shirt and a darker grey tie completed the outfit.

'Briony!' He moved quickly towards her, his hand outstretched. 'I hope you didn't mind this arrangement being made in your absence? You look charming,' he went on before she could think of any suitable reply. If it hadn't been ridiculous for a man of his age and sophistication, she would have thought he was nervous, too. Still talking, he steered her towards the door and, before she'd had time to collect her wits, she was sitting in his car, an old but immaculately maintained silver Rolls-Royce.

'Wh-where are we going?' was all she could think of to say.

'There's a very good restaurant on the outskirts of Barnstaple. I've reserved a table. They have a cabaret on Friday evenings and a dance. You *do* dance?' he asked anxiously.

'Yes,' Briony said faintly. He must think her an absolute drip, with no social conversation. But events were moving too swiftly for her. She'd barely got used to the idea of dining with him when she found she would also have to dance with him. The thought of it, the idea of being held close to that lean, rangy body, was playing havoc with her nerves.

'Good!' He didn't seem to have noticed anything untoward.

He was an excellent driver. Briony's eyes were drawn irresistibly to his hands, relaxed but always in command of the steering-wheel. They were strong, capable-looking hands, slightly roughened by short, dark hair. Briony recalled how they had felt when she'd flown at him and he'd grasped her wrists. Unable to control the involuntary reaction, she shivered. Slight though it was, it did not escape his notice.

'Warm enough?'

'Oh—yes—thank you.' Snap out of it, she urged herself. Think of something *intelligent* to say. But, though she racked her brains, not a single topic recommended itself to her.

'You're not annoyed?' he said, then saved her the necessity of asking what he meant, by adding, 'You're very quiet. Perhaps you didn't want to come out with me?'

'Oh, yes. I mean—no, I'm not annoyed. And thank you very much for asking me.' You sound like a teenager on her first date instead of a mature woman, she told herself despairingly.

'That's all right, then.' Briefly, one of his hands covered one of hers.

Oh, lord, Briony thought. How was she to get through this evening without betraying the confused upheaval within her?

The restaurant was an excellent choice. Briony had never been there before. In fact, though she and Promilla had been in Devon for more than two years now, there had been little time for socialising or exploring the surrounding countryside. Most of their contacts were business ones, and their search had been for shops rather than restaurants—outlets for their work.

Teale gave their order for steak with a side salad, and chose an appropriate wine.

'I don't drink,' Briony protested as he filled her glass. 'Honestly, I'd much rather have water.'

'This isn't drinking!' he teased. 'A little of this won't hurt you. It sharpens the appetite.'

Her appetite certainly *needed* sharpening, Briony thought wryly. She didn't feel a bit hungry; she was too nervous. In a way, it was reassuring to find that she *could* still feel this way. It was recapturing for her the delightful lost teenage years when every new date was an adventure. She recalled the exciting will-he-won't-he-kiss-me speculation in which she and her friends had always indulged. The thought brought her up sharply. Would Teale expect to kiss her after this evening? Should she let him? But she wasn't allowed much time for nervous conjecture.

'Now, tell me about yourself.'

'Goodness!' she said involuntarily. 'I wouldn't know where to start!'

'Has your life been *that* eventful?' His grey eyes were laughing at her. It was amazing how a change of mood had affected their colour. They were no longer a cold shade of steel, but warm and alive, with a darker ring of grey around the iris. Briony suddenly realised how intently she was staring into those eyes and dropped her gaze to her plate.

'It's just that I don't know what you'd find interesting,' she told him.

'Well, for a start, what are you doing in Devon? You're not local?'

'No——' she ventured to look at him again '—I was born in Essex. The nearest town of any size was Saffron Walden. My father was a farmer.'

'A wealthy one, or an impoverished one?' And, as a look of pain disturbed Briony's face, 'I'm sorry. That smacks of impertinence.'

'Oh, no. It's just that he *was* quite well-to-do once. But he made some bad investments and lost all his money. It's when things like that happen,' she said with a trace of bitterness, 'that you find out whether people are really fond of you for your own sake.'

'A man?' Teale hazarded, and as she nodded he reached across the table and took one of her hands. 'Never mind,' he said comfortingly, 'better to find out before it's too late.'

'Yes,' she agreed. The trouble was that in some ways it had already been too late. But Briony didn't want to bore someone like Teale Munro with the shadows from her past. Quickly, she reverted to her presence in Devon, briefly outlining her long friendship with Promilla, their decision to go into partnership and make a break from their former surroundings. 'Munro doesn't sound like a Devonshire name?' She was eager to know more about him, too.

'No. My parents came from Stirlingshire. But they settled here, and my sister and I were born here.'

'Are you and your sister alike?'

He laughed. It was an engaging sound and Briony watched, mesmerised, all her attention riveted on his face as it broke up into lines and clefts that emphasised his craggy attraction.

'Facially, we're very alike. But I'm nearly six foot and she's hardly any taller than you. Anyway, we're supposed to be talking about *you*. Have you any brothers and sisters?'

'No, I was an only child. And both my parents are dead now. My father died two years ago.' Remembered sadness clouded her piquant little face again. Though she and her father hadn't been all that close, she'd missed him, and his death had precipitated an unhappy train of events.

'And you've no one else?' Teale interrupted her train of thought.

She hesitated, then said, 'My only living relative is in France.' She said it with deliberate casualness. She didn't want to talk about her ownership or lack of a family any further. It was too personal a subject to discuss with a total stranger.

Briony allowed herself to be persuaded to a second slice of gâteau. As they talked, Teale had kept filling up her glass and she felt pleasantly relaxed and not a little woozy. She was surprised to find that she'd cleared her plate. It must have been the wine, she mused.

While coffee was being served, the cabaret began, two men and two girls singing popular songs. It was nothing pretentious and lasted just long enough not to become tedious. Briony felt so at ease with Teale now that she did not experience the slightest flicker of alarm when he stood up and invited her to dance.

But, once she was in his arms, it was a very different matter.

CHAPTER THREE

'RELAX, Briony!' Teale's hand tightened on her waist. 'You're as tense as the day you decided to use me as a punchbag. We're friends now—I hope?'

'Yes. I'm sorry, I expect it's because I haven't been dancing for some while.' Briony knew it wasn't that. It was the closeness of his hard, vital body, the brush of his legs against hers, the intense sexual awareness, the effort to repress the betraying shivers that threatened to course along her spine.

He seemed to accept her excuse.

'Then we must see to it that you get more practice. I like to dance, don't you?'

'Yes, very much.' The words came out on a breathless note, as though she'd been running instead of moving in this slow, drugging way around the floor. Her awareness of him physically was increasing with every minute. Her heart was thudding so loudly that she wondered he was not aware of it.

There was little room to manoeuvre on the small dance-floor, but Briony didn't object to the crush. They danced every dance and she let Teale guide her round the floor. She was wrapped in a mysterious, drowsy sweetness, totally given up to the sensations that engulfed her, arousing wanton emotions inside her. She didn't want the evening to end, so it was with a sense of deeply felt deprivation that she realised the last waltz was over and Teale was leading her from the floor.

'Not too tired, I hope?' he asked as he eased into the driving seat of the Rolls-Royce.

'Not a bit.' The languor that possessed her was not fatigue.

'Good. It's such a beautiful night, I thought we'd drive along the coast. I never tire of looking at the sea.'

Briony knew she was letting her imagination run rampant. But she was picturing that drive, seeing the car stopping, overlooking some isolated bay, Teale turning towards her. She was imagining his lips crushing her own, kissing her with the hunger and urgency of male appetite. And she knew she wouldn't object. She was filled with an aching longing to be back in the intoxication of his arms.

Teale engaged first gear and the car glided smoothly away.

'I feel I owe you some explanation about my behaviour towards Matthew, about Matthew himself,' he said, breaking in on her mood of dreamy euphoria. 'And it's not the kind of thing you can talk about in a public restaurant.'

Briony felt disappointment swamp her. He only wanted to talk, while she wanted so much more. Her readiness to be swayed by him was disturbing. It was a long time since any man had affected her in this way. She wasn't sure she *had* ever known such intense physical sensations. This man stirred every nerve she possessed. Her brain fought a desperate battle to keep control over her body and to concentrate on what he was saying.

'You don't have to explain,' she said. 'It's obviously a family matter.'

'I'd *like* to tell you,' Teale persisted. 'You see, last week was the first time any of us had seen Matthew for several years. He'd just disappeared into the blue as far as we were concerned. He went off without a word. Rhoda was devastated. She still loves him, in spite of everything.'

'You can't just forget all those years of marriage,' Briony pointed out. 'There are so many shared memories. Are there any children?'

'Three. Two boys and a girl, seventeen, sixteen and fifteen. It hasn't been easy for Rhoda these last few years, bringing them up on her own.'

'Matthew implied that *you'd* never approved of him.'

'I didn't, I still don't. He's turned out exactly as my father predicted. At twenty-two he was a no-hoper, and he's still a no-hoper. Oh, I know you think he's got talent. You're probably right. I've never claimed he wasn't intelligent. But he'll never put it to any good use.'

'How did they meet?'

'At art school. He looked and behaved much the same then as he does now: the long hair, the beard, the irresponsible character. At twenty-two, it was an image practically every art student cultivated. But at forty—well, it's just plain ridiculous.'

Briony could see that it *would* be totally incomprehensible to Teale. His own appearance was conventional, even when wearing casual clothes. And he was obviously well-off. She wondered where his money came from, whether it was inherited or whether he followed some profession. But she didn't like to ask.

'Where does your sister live?'

'These days, she lives in a cottage on part of my property. I can help her a bit now. When she was first married, I couldn't—I was still making my own way. And, even if I'd been able to, Matthew wouldn't have accepted help from me. From women,' a note of anger crept into his voice, 'yes; from me, no.'

'He must have sensed your disapproval even then,' Briony said diffidently.

The car slowed and pulled off the road, nosing up to the rail at the cliff edge. Teale switched off the engine and turned towards her, his arm sliding along the back of the seat behind her head. Needles of excitement pricked her skin, but he didn't attempt to touch her.

'Look, Briony, I know you think I'm hard on Rawlinson. But he's married to my sister. If he weren't, he could live how he liked. I knew the first time I clapped eyes on him that he wouldn't be able to support her. I also suspected he'd end up breaking her heart. And I was right. That's why I was so furious when I thought he was having an affair with you. It wouldn't have been the first time.'

'Doesn't he care for his wife and children?'

'God knows what Matthew cares for; I don't.'

'He cares about his painting,' Briony said thoughtfully. 'Perhaps, if he could make a success of that...'

'I don't think he wants to be a success. It's much less effort to be a failure. But that brings us into the realms of psychology, and it's much too nice a night for that.' He seemed to deliberately shake off his mood, his tone lightening. 'But don't let's waste any more of this evening on Matthew. Feel like a walk?'

'Yes.' Anything to prolong their time together, she thought.

There was a full moon hanging like an enormous lantern over the sea. Briony slipped off her high heels and, at Teale's urging, she also removed her tights.

'Otherwise you'll ruin them,' he said practically, 'and, besides, it's much more fun to paddle barefoot.'

The last thing she had expected was that Teale would find enjoyment in such an unsophisticated pursuit, that he would roll up the immaculate trouser legs of his suit. The way he'd been talking about Matthew, she would have expected this to be far too unconventional for him.

The tide was out and the moonlight was reflected in the long stretches of wet sand and shallow water. For a while, they strolled along in harmonious silence. Briony found herself wondering whimsically if there were nights when there was magic in the air. It seemed to her that she'd never felt a greater exaltation of spirits, a keener awareness of the beauty of her surroundings. She would have liked to share this thought with Teale. But she suspected her feelings were not unrelated to his presence here with her.

Their moods must have been closely attuned, however, for suddenly he said, 'It's an especially lovely night. I suppose we all have a particular fondness for the place where we were born and grew up, but for me this piece of coastline is unsurpassed. It has such infinite variety.'

'Yes,' Briony agreed. 'It can be fierce or gentle.' Like Teale himself, she thought yearningly.

'Mmmn, but the gentleness is deceptive.' For a startled moment, she thought he must have read her mind, but then he went on, 'Morte Point, just north of here, is notoriously dangerous to shipping. Did you know these sands are reputed to be haunted by the victims of wreckers? Apparently it used to be the local custom to tie lanterns to the tails of cows. Unsuspecting captains were lured into what seemed to be a harbour, with the lights of ships swinging at anchor. The human race can be very cruel to its own kind.' There was a trace of bitterness in the words, and Briony hastily sought to dispel the mood.

'I wish I *did* know more about Devonshire,' she said. 'But we always seem to be so busy. I've done a bit of sketching and painting in Gwinvercombe itself, but that's all.'

'A pity,' he agreed, 'when there are so many beauty spots to see. Have you never been to Clovelly, for instance?'

'No. I haven't even got that far.'

'Would you like to go?'

'With you?' she asked involuntarily, then felt herself blushing. He probably hadn't meant that.

'If you'll do me the honour? And if you can spare a day? Next week, perhaps?'

'I'd like that,' she admitted. 'But can *you* spare the time? You must be busy, too?'

As a hint, it had been a failure, she thought later. She had been hoping Teale would tell her what *he* did for a living. But he volunteered nothing beyond the remark that he expected to have some free time in the next week or so. Despite their evening together, she felt she'd learned very little about him. And she was no nearer to discovering exactly what it was about him that fascinated her. It was partly physical, of course. She had no doubt of his masculine potency. But she'd already known that. His dark looks, too, were attractive. Several times throughout the evening her pulses had stirred in response to a glance or a smile from him. But their knowledge of each other was all superficial. Their conversation had been based on generalities. All she could confidently assert was that Teale Munro was thirty-eight, intelligent and well spoken, with a sense of humour she had not expected. But then, she admitted ruefully, there were things she hadn't told him about herself. Things she was chary of telling him yet. Perhaps some day. If their friendship flourished.

He hadn't attempted to kiss her at parting, and she had experienced strong disappointment. She was disappointed, too, that he hadn't asked to see her at the weekend.

'The Munros would have stopped me marrying their daughter if they could,' Matthew volunteered suddenly the following Tuesday. 'They didn't like the fact that I hadn't got a "proper job".' He and Briony had been working on opposite sides of the studio, and Matthew had stopped to ease his cramped muscles. She was careful not to interrupt his unexpected burst of confidentiality and he went on, 'But Rhoda, bless her, stuck to her guns and finally old Munro offered me a job at his office in Exeter. I suppose he thought he was doing me a favour,' Matthew conceded. And, with a slight shudder, 'He was a solicitor. Tied to a desk from nine till five, working over dry-as-dust books, even dustier papers. Wills, lawsuits. Depressing. I stuck it as long as I could. But it was too stultifying. I jacked it in.' He returned to his painting, and Briony assumed that was all he intended to say.

She returned to the outline she was working on. It was a painting of a man set against a background of Devonshire coastline. She tried to tell herself it was entirely a product of her imagination but, as the details grew beneath her skilful brush, the man's lean, swarthy face took on more and more of the likeness of Teale Munro. She was so absorbed that she was unaware Matthew had broken off work again.

'He doesn't need women, you know.' He had moved to stand behind her. 'Oh, I'm sure he's got the normal healthy male appetites. But he doesn't understand women. He couldn't understand Rhoda wanting to marry me. He didn't understand Charley. And he won't understand you, either, Briony. The strange thing is that all three of you have a lot in common. If you're wise, you won't let him hurt *you*.'

'Charley? Who's Charley?' For a moment, Briony ignored the rest.

'Charlene, his wife.'

'You said he wasn't married!' Briony accused. For the life of her, she couldn't repress the note of shock and Matthew looked at her significantly.

'His *ex*-wife,' he said with emphasis. 'They've been divorced some time now.'

Briony breathed again.

'Were there any children?'

'One—a boy. Charley got custody. Munro didn't contest it. Most of the time, he didn't seem to realise Charley and the boy existed. And he had the temerity to call *me* a selfish swine!'

'Doesn't Teale ever see his son, then?' It was more than idle curiosity that made Briony ask.

'When he's in London, I believe. He's got a flat there that he uses for part of the year.'

That evening, Briony repeated the conversation—the longest she'd ever had with Matthew—to Promilla.

'Perhaps Matthew's right. Perhaps I *should* steer clear of Teale Munro. I don't want to get hurt again. It's taken me two years to get over...'

Promilla paused in her sewing. She always had some work in hand.

'You can't spend the rest of your life in a vacuum,' she told Briony. 'You're too young to cut men out of your life altogether. I rather like what I've seen of Teale Munro. I think you owe it to him to give him a chance—and not to take him at anyone else's assessment.'

'Including yours?' Briony asked drily.

'I know you won't believe me but, just because one marriage failed, it doesn't mean another will.'

'Slow down, Prom! I hadn't got as far as thinking about marrying the man.'

Promilla looked disbelieving, but she let the comment pass.

'Did Matthew tell you any more about himself? What did he do after he left his father-in-law's business?' she asked instead.

'A variety of things. None of them lasted very long. He didn't like the discipline of regular hours or office life. He still had the urge to make some kind of career from his art. But his in-laws pooh-poohed it. Finally, he gave up conventional work and he and his wife went in for self-sufficiency. You know, growing their own food, keeping livestock.'

'Not the action of a lazy man,' Promilla said.

'No. And it couldn't have been very profitable. His wife must be a real brick. She went along with him every step of the way. He obviously thinks the world of her. So what I can't understand is why he should suddenly leave her and disappear for years.'

'Didn't Teale say something about Matthew having an affair? A man can still be tempted even if he *does* love his wife. Perhaps he went off with the other woman?' Promilla put down her sewing with a tired sigh. 'I'll be glad to get some extra help. It will give you a bit more time for your painting, too. I've put an advertisement in the local paper and in *Devon Life*. Let's hope we get a quick response.'

'Clovelly hasn't changed much over the years.' Teale said it with satisfaction.

Briony had spent several days in a fever of impatience, waiting for his call.

'Friday was the earliest I could make it,' he'd told her apologetically when finally he'd telephoned. 'I had a job which had to be finished by a certain date. I've been working all day and half the night as it is to see it through.'

She would have enjoyed going anywhere in Teale's company, Briony thought, but she had to admit that Clovelly was especially delightful on that mid-September morning. Gift shops and car parks, which so often spoilt the atmosphere of beauty spots, were kept well out of sight above the little village. No cars drove up and down the steep cobbled street with its white cascade of houses, simply because it was impossible to do so.

'They use sleds to carry provisions throughout the year,' Teale told her. 'The donkeys are brought out in the summer, but largely for the benefit of visitors. Clovelly gets half a million tourists in summer.'

'Are most of them here today?' she asked wryly, and was rewarded by seeing his lean face break into the attractive smile which always made her heart perform incredible gymnastics.

'Come again in winter,' he advised. 'It comes into its own again then, as tranquil as it must have been in the days before tourism.'

He hadn't said 'come again with me', she thought, then rebuked herself for presumptuousness. Why should he?

'There's some disagreement over the name Clovelly,' he told her as they descended the hill. 'Some say it comes from the Latin *clausa vallis*—a closed glen. Others think that as *cleave* was the Saxon for cliff, cleave-valley might be another derivation. Again, it could be a corruption of *cleave-leigh*, the cliff place, as its manor was called in the Domesday Book.'

Briony was delighted to find that Teale shared her interest in folklore and legend. Among other legends about the village, he related for her that of the Gregg family who had inhabited a cave near Mouth Mill and made a living by robbing lonely travellers.

'Their food came from the same source,' he told her. 'The limbs of the people they murdered and pickled. They were cannibals. Incredibly, this went on for twenty-five years, until one of their victims escaped and gave the alarm.'

This tale elicited the shudder that was intended, but such gruesome histories were quickly forgotten in the natural beauty of Clovelly.

'I *must* come here to paint,' Briony exclaimed as they reached the harbour, where a row of houses leant over the pebbled beach. On the jutting jetty were bollards reputed to be Spanish cannon salvaged after the Armada.

Modern town-planners should come to Clovelly, Briony thought. Not one house was the same as the other. Yet there was a symmetry as they overlapped and tumbled down the cliff. To say she must paint a place was the highest accolade Briony could give. Now she was at a loss for superlatives.

'Pretty, isn't it?' Teale agreed.

But pretty was an inadequate word with which to describe Clovelly, Briony thought. It was a rarer quality than that. It had an atmosphere that was singularly Mediterranean, and yet at the same time completely English.

'Talking of painting, have you thought any more about showing Matthew's work to an expert?' Teale asked. She was surprised by his interest.

'I've thought about it a lot. But Matthew won't hear of it.'

'Suppose you were to send one up to London without saying anything. Would he notice one was missing?'

'Probably not,' Briony admitted. 'He's done so many. And he never looks at them again anyway once they're finished.'

Teale had brought a picnic lunch which they ate on the front overlooking the sea. Wheeling gulls swooped and complained above their heads, while smaller birds such as sparrows reaped the harvest of crumbs.

'There would have been a very different atmosphere at the beginning of the last century,' Teale mused as they watched the meandering tourists with their cameras. 'Once, this was a thriving fishing village. Local cod was alleged to be the best in the world. But the most plentiful catch was the famous Clovelly herring. It's said that sometimes the nets were so full there was no time to remove the fish as they were hauled on board. Instead they had to be towed into harbour with the fish still enmeshed. But then suddenly the herring moved elsewhere.'

Teale reverted to the subject of Matthew's paintings once more as they repacked the picnic basket.

'Would you permit me to take one of his pictures, next time I go up to London?'

'Why on earth would you bother to do that?' Briony asked with more frankness than tact. 'I thought you had no time for Matthew?'

'But I do have a lot of time for my sister,' Teale pointed out gently, apparently unoffended. 'And, if there's a chance Matthew is finally going to make something of himself, it would be to her benefit, wouldn't it?'

'They're back together again?' Briony *had* wondered.

'As if they'd never been apart. And, as far as I can make out, she's never even asked him where he'd been or why.' Teale sounded incredulous.

'I couldn't do that,' Briony said positively.

'Nor I, but Rhoda is rather unique.'

'She sounds very nice,' Briony agreed wistfully. She wondered if Teale would ever invite her to meet his sister.

They made the climb back to the car, with Briony protesting laughingly at the steepness. Teale held out his hand, offering to pull her up the incline, and at his touch a sweet glow flowed through her breast. It seemed to run throughout the whole of her body from head to foot. If his merest touch could affect her this way, what on earth would it be like if he were ever to make love to her? Briony was glad her disordered breathing could be attributed to the stiffness of the ascent.

'When are you seeing Teale again?' Promilla served her friend with a generous helping of curry, a once-a-week meal in their establishment. Fortunately, Briony enjoyed it as much as her friend.

'I don't know, Prom,' she said regretfully. 'He didn't make any arrangements. He just dropped me off at the door, thanked me for a nice day and that was it.'

'Has he kissed you yet?'

'No. I wish...Oh!' Impatiently, she brushed aside the longings that beset her every time she saw or thought of Teale Munro. 'For heaven's sake, let's talk about something else. Prom,' she looked doubtfully at her friend, 'since you said you didn't mind, I've written to Iseult and asked her to come over for Christmas. Is that OK?'

'Of course. It'll be nice for you.' Promilla pulled a chair up to the table. 'Christmas *is* a family time, after all.' She spoke a little absently and Briony looked sharply at her, wondering if her friend did have some objection after all, or if she was thinking of her own lack of family. But then Promilla went on, 'I had a phone call in answer to my advertisement while you were out. It sounds very promising. I took a note of the address and said I'd go over on Monday and look at specimens of this woman's work. It's easier than for her to bring it all here. The only thing is, I've double-booked myself. Sukie Wareing is coming over on Monday with a couple of clients.'

'Well, that's no problem surely? You could ring the woman back and say you'll interview her another day.'

'She was ringing from a call-box, and I can't remember her name.' That was unlike the meticulous Promilla. 'I was wondering if you'd go and see her for me.'

'But I don't know anything about sewing,' Briony objected.

'You know enough to be able to judge the quality. Do say you'll go. The sooner we get someone, the better for both of us. Especially,' teasingly, 'if you're going to be taking your day off in future.' Until latterly, both girls had worked a six-day week. Briony's weekday outing with Teale had been an unprecedented event.

'I might not be having any more days off,' Briony said pessimistically. 'But all right, I'll go and see this woman.

You sure you can't remember her name? It'll be a bit awkward.'

The Monday appointment had been made for three o'clock. Briony drove inland, glad of the opportunity to get away from the shop. As usual, it had been a quiet morning and, though Matthew was working harder than ever, he still did not appear on Mondays.

Leaving Gwinvercombe, the winding secretive lanes were green tunnels where boughs met overhead. In spring, the lanes around the old town glittered with wild flowers. And summer had brought its own colourful crop—daisies, purple globe thistles and yellow-horned poppies. At first, the road climbed away from the seaside town, through wild-blossoming valleys and old hill-perched villages. But soon, as though drawn by some irresistible force, the road returned to the coastline, flanked by windswept downs on one side and marshy meadows on the other. Briony had not been in this direction before and she gave a little gasp of pleasure as the road opened out on to a magnificent prospect of sea and sky.

She had to enquire her way once or twice, but finally she found herself bumping along an unmade track towards a long, low building just visible through the surrounding trees. The spot was as isolated as if marooned on a desert island. A large but neat garden surrounded the cottage. At one side she could see a line of hen coops, and two tethered goats grazed placidly on the front lawn.

'I'm Briony Kent,' she told the slim dark-haired woman who came to the door. 'I'm from the Blue Unicorn in Gwinvercombe. It's about the advertisement for an assistant craft worker.'

'Strange,' the woman's broad intelligent brow wrinkled, 'I thought the lady I spoke to had some kind of foreign name.'

'That was my partner, Promilla Kadri. It's a Pakistani name.' Briony explained her friend's absence as she followed the woman inside the low-beamed cottage.

It was much larger inside than she'd imagined, and simply furnished, as though the woman were not very well-to-do. But it was spotlessly clean, with freshly whitened roughcast walls and gleaming floorboards. There were evidences everywhere of the woman's skill with her needle—embroidered tablecloths, chairbacks, patchwork cushions, collages.

'I make my own curtains and loose covers, too,' the woman said, following her gaze.

'I don't think there's any doubt that you're just what my friend's looking for,' Briony told her as she took the proffered seat. 'I believe she told you the rates she'd be prepared to pay? All we need to know is how many hours you can give us and on what days?'

'You'd expect me to come into Gwinvercombe, to the shop?' The woman sounded dismayed.

'Well, yes! We need extra help with serving in the shop as well.'

'I thought I'd be able to do the work at home. I've no transport.'

Briony thought quickly. It would be a pity to lose this woman's services. They might never find anyone else as good.

'Would you be prepared to come in if you *did* have transport?'

'Yes, but . . .'

'You're not too far from Gwinvercombe here.' The other woman's expression brightened as Briony said, 'How would it be if I came out and fetched you?'

'That would be marvellous! But wouldn't it be an awful nuisance? Especially in winter?'

'It might be sometimes,' Briony said with her usual frankness, 'but,' she smiled, 'it will be worth it to have your help.'

'You'll have a cup of tea?' the woman pressed. 'We don't get many visitors out here, and it's rather lonely now my two older children have left home.'

'How many have you? Will it be a problem leaving them?'

'There's only one left at home. She's at school all day. Besides, she's turned fifteen now. Old enough to look after herself. I wish you could have met her—and my husband. But he has a regular appointment every Monday.'

'I've just realised,' Briony said, a mouthwatering home-made scone half-way to her mouth, 'I don't even know your name. My partner couldn't remember...'

'That's very odd! When I told her, she said it was a name she wasn't likely to forget in a hurry. In fact, I wondered what she meant.' She held out her hand and smiled. 'Better late than never. I'm Rhoda Rawlinson.'

Briony dropped her scone, then spent several minutes apologising profusely as she picked up the crumbs. She needed the time with her flushed face bent over her task to recover from the shock. She'd thought the woman's face was oddly familiar, but assumed she'd seen her before somewhere. Perhaps in Gwinvercombe on market day. But now she realised the familiarity had been Rhoda Rawlinson's likeness to her brother. The grey eyes, with their darker-ringed irises were exactly the same shape as his, though of a slightly warmer hue. Why hadn't Rhoda recognised *her* name? Oh, heavens! Suppose Matthew *hadn't* told his wife everything? Suppose Rhoda came to work for the Blue Unicorn and met her husband there? Could Promilla have overlooked such an essential point? For Briony realised now that her visit to Rhoda

Rawlinson was a put-up job on her partner's part. She must find out just what the other woman knew.

'I'm sorry, I didn't realise. You're Teale Munro's sister?'

'Yes,' Rhoda Rawlinson looked puzzled. 'You know my brother? Oh...of course.' Enlightenment illuminated her lovely face. 'I didn't connect, but it must be... A craft shop in Gwinvercombe. You have an artists' studio there as well? Where my husband does his painting? I thought I'd heard the name Briony just recently.'

Briony let out a careful breath of relief.

'Your husband's very talented.'

'I know,' Rhoda said simply. 'I just wish *he* thought so. I'm very grateful for all the help you've given him. Just wait,' she said gleefully, 'till I tell him we're to be working under the same roof.'

Briony just hoped Matthew would approve.

'I never fail to be surprised at people's goodness,' Rhoda said as she showed Briony around the rest of the cottage. 'Take this place, for example. It belongs to my brother. He offered it to me a few years ago when...' She stopped, a slight quiver in her voice, then went on, 'When things weren't going too well for me and the kids. He wouldn't take any rent for it. But now Matthew's...' Again she stopped. 'But, now I'm getting a job, I'll be able to offer him some part of it.'

Briony wondered if, now Matthew was home, he was objecting to living off his brother-in-law's charity and if that was why Rhoda needed a job. Her admiration for Teale's sister was growing by leaps and bounds. She had enjoyed meeting her and had stayed much longer than she'd intended, she realised.

'Goodness! I must get back to the shop. Promilla will be wanting to know the outcome of our meeting. Can I tell her you'll start next week?'

As the car bumped and jolted back down the rutted approach, Briony was disconcerted to see another vehicle coming towards her. There was very little room to pass and she didn't want to end up in the ditch that flanked the track. The Rolls-Royce began to back, its driver flashing his lights at her to advance. Thankfully, she did so. Then she recognised the car. It was Teale's. She hadn't expected to encounter him, especially since Rhoda had said there was another entrance to his property, a made-up drive that led up to the big house. The Rolls reversed into a concealed gateway and she saw that he was getting out. Unaccountably, she stalled her engine.

'Briony?' He leant in at the window and Briony caught a hint of the cologne he used. There was a note of enquiry in his voice. She thought he did not seem altogether pleased to see her. 'What are you doing here?'

'I've been to see your sister.'

'Why?' he demanded sharply.

'I didn't know she *was* your sister at first.' Hastily, Briony explained her presence. It had struck her that Teale might think she'd come here in the hope of seeing him. And, while she was ridiculously glad they *had* met, her pride would never have allowed her to go in search of him.

'Rhoda wants a job?' he said incredulously. 'But there's no need for that. Or for you and your friend to help her. She knows I'll always...'

'I got the impression she'd like a break from the house and a bit of independence. And it's not a question of *us* helping *her*. Her work is really excellent. We'll be only too pleased to give her as much work as she can handle.' Shyly, she added, 'She's nice, Teale. I like her.' And, as he nodded, as if that was only to be expected, she said, 'I'd better get on.' She restarted her engine, reluctantly admitting to herself that this encounter was not proving to be a successful one and that it would be as well to end it.

'When's the best time for me to come in and collect one of Matthew's pictures?'

Reprieved, she answered eagerly, 'It'll have to be at a weekend, or on a Monday. I can't guarantee he won't be around another day.'

'This weekend, then? Saturday evening? I'm afraid I can't manage any other time.'

She nodded happily. At least then she was certain of seeing him again. Her mood of euphoria lasted for the first few miles of the return journey. Perhaps Teale would be in a more approachable mood by the weekend. He'd seemed a bit prickly today. His manner was almost absent, as if his mind were on other more important things. Which wasn't very flattering. Face it, she told herself, her spirits drooping again, he took you out a couple of times to make up for his insulting manner towards you. He probably feels he's squared the account now.

And, talking of squaring accounts...

'Promilla Kadri! I've got a bone to pick with you! You knew exactly who you were sending me to see! What do you think you're playing at?'

'Are you furious?' Promilla looked up guiltily as Briony levied her accusation.

'I ought to be!' Briony sighed. 'But no, I'm not.' She collapsed into the chair kept for customers. 'Just amazed that you could be so devious.'

'I thought it was a good opportunity for you to meet Teale's sister and get another view of the situation.'

'Yes, I *am* glad I've met Rhoda, and she'll be a tremendous asset.' Briony told her friend the terms of their agreement. '*And* I bumped into Teale. I suppose,' ironically, 'you weren't hoping for that as well?'

Promilla shrugged plump shoulders, her round face mischievously creased. 'It was always on the cards. Did it do any good?'

'Not in the way you mean. He's coming over Saturday evening. But it's not really to see me.'

'You don't *know* that,' Promilla pointed out after she'd heard Teale's plans for Matthew's work. 'The painting could be just an excuse.'

'I wish I could think so, but I don't. Teale's only interest, so far as I can see, is in helping his sister. There's a special bond between twins they say.'

Nevertheless, this did not stop Briony looking forward to Saturday evening with nervous anticipation. She'd been on edge all week, unable to concentrate on her painting. It was only excitement on Matthew's behalf, she tried telling herself, the hope that his work would receive the recognition it richly deserved.

At five-thirty, she closed up the shop and went through to the kitchen. Normally at this time of day Promilla was at the cooker, preparing high tea. Instead, she emerged from her bedroom wearing a light raincoat.

'All right if I take the car? You won't be wanting it?'

'Where on earth are you going?' Promilla never went out in the evening. She much preferred to sit in front of the television, dividing her time between the programmes and her sewing.

'I'm going into Ilfracombe. Remember I told you, Sukie Wareing is taking me to see the customer who was here the other day? I'm to plan a whole colour scheme for her bedroom.'

'I thought she said that would do any time. Why tonight? Promilla, you're up to something!' Briony realized. 'You're going out deliberately, because Teale's coming.' A little desperately, she pleaded, 'There's no need to be tactful. He'll probably only be here five minutes.'

'Who's being tactful?' Promilla retorted. 'Can't I have a Saturday evening out if I feel like it? Are you turning into some sort of slave-driver?'

Briony wasn't a bit deceived, and she watched her partner's departure with a mixture of affection and amused exasperation. It wouldn't be her friend's fault if she didn't end up in Teale Munro's arms. She shivered at the thought.

She'd told Promilla that Teale would probably be there five minutes. Nevertheless, she took as much care over her appearance as if he would be spending several hours with her. The September evenings were growing cool, but it was too soon for fires, so she settled for hip-hugging black slacks and a fluffy angora sweater whose blue matched her eyes and whose softness emphasised her deceptively fragile femininity.

Even though she was expecting Teale, the doorbell made Briony jump and she nearly dropped the cup she was drying. She hadn't felt like eating a substantial meal and she'd settled for cheese on toast and a pot of tea. She counted to ten and made herself move slowly to the door, even when the bell pealed another urgent summons.

'Hello.' He stepped inside briskly, bringing a breath of damp sea air with him. The scent mingled with his cologne. Briony felt overpowered by his height and proximity. She moved hastily aside. 'It's raining,' he told her. 'I was beginning to think you weren't in, after all. That you'd forgotten I was coming.' As if she could!

She bolted the door and led the way up to the studio, acutely aware of him following close behind her. She'd set Matthew's paintings out in a long line.

'I got them ready for you. There are several more since the last time you looked. They get better and better. Oh,

I do hope you can interest the gallery in them.' She realised her voice was too high. She was gabbling nervously and he was looking at her rather oddly.

After careful consideration, Teale selected two. One was a large still life of fruit and flowers. It was the one Briony would have chosen herself. It wasn't the latest, but it was certainly the best of Matthew's recent efforts. From the early days of thick, swirling paint, he had progressed to a slightly more serene brush movements. But his style was still very distinctive, his use of reds still predominant. She wasn't sure why Teale had chosen the other. It was one of the first Matthew had done, a disturbing abstract of swirling primary colours that captured yet tortured the eye. But when she questioned Teale he merely looked vague and said he just had a hunch about it.

Briony provided cardboard corners to protect the frames, and preceded Teale as he carried the pictures downstairs. Following her intuition, she headed straight for the outer door and was surprised when he did not immediately follow her. She turned round to look at him and saw him regarding her quizzically.

'In a hurry to be rid of me? Are you very busy this evening?'

'No, not really. That is...no busier than usual. I mean...'

'What's wrong, Briony?' He leant the paintings against the counter and came towards her. He stood so close that she was hard put to it not to retreat. Gently, he asked, 'Have I annoyed you again in some way?'

'Of course not.' She plucked nervously at the fluffy sleeve of her sweater. 'I just thought... Well, you only came for the pictures, didn't you?'

'Is *that* what's offended you?' He sounded amused. 'Because you thought...'

'I'm not in the least offended! Why should I be?' But she *was* hurt, quite unreasonably so, she reminded herself. Their acquaintance was of the most casual kind.

'Oh, Briony!' His tone was gently mocking now. 'You're a very bad liar.'

CHAPTER FOUR

'YOU'RE a very bad liar,' Teale repeated. 'You *are* offended! Did you really think I'd just walk out with these pictures under my arm? Naturally, I've been waiting for you to invite me in for a coffee.'

Briony looked at him doubtfully. He could just be saying that, to spare her feelings.

Teale misinterpreted her misgivings. 'What is it, Briony? Is Promilla out? You're alone? I can assure you, a coffee *is* all I had in mind.'

'I realise that!' she said indignantly. 'And I hardly think I need a chaperone. You're very welcome to a coffee if you can really spare the time.'

She led the way through to the living quarters, remembering the annoyance she'd felt at his uninvited invasion; was it only a month ago? Strange how the situation had changed in so short a space of time.

Teale eased his lean length down on to a couch which was artistically draped with bright blue, yellow and red Iranian *kilims*. He looked around the terracotta-painted room appreciatively.

'This room has tremendous individuality. It's very colourful.' And, as Tara the Siamese strolled towards him and sniffed disdainfully at his shoe, he remarked, 'I see you like cats. Me too—any animals, in fact. You two girls certainly have the gift of home-making. Rhoda has the knack, too. She'd like this room.'

'I hope she'll be seeing it soon,' Briony told him. 'She starts work here on Monday.'

71

'Yes. I wanted to talk to you about that—among other things.'

'Oh?' Briony regarded him warily. Did he still disapprove of his sister being employed at the Blue Unicorn?

'Mmm. There's absolutely no need for you to pick Rhoda up every morning. She can use my car most days and, failing that, I'll drive her to the nearest bus stop.'

'That would be a help,' Briony admitted. She went into the kitchen and switched on the percolator. 'Now and again we oversleep, and even though we live on the premises we only get into the shop on time by the skin of our teeth. I suppose it's because we keep such late hours,' she told him. She hovered in the communicating doorway, unable to relax. 'Sometimes, if a painting's going well, I'll work until two or three in the morning.' She realised from Teale's quizzical expression that she was talking too much again.

'Come and sit down while the coffee perks,' he told her. 'I can't talk to you when you're flitting in and out of the kitchen like that.' He indicated a place beside him on the couch and Briony swallowed nervously as she obeyed. 'Why,' he said almost to himself, 'do I feel this continual compulsion to explain myself to you? Even though I have very rational reasons for what must seem to you my irrational dislike of Matthew Rawlinson.' His grey eyes appraised her small, heart-shaped face. His gaze rested for a long moment on the full, soft lips of her generous mouth and Briony was afraid he would notice their responsive quiver.

'I haven't *asked* you to explain anything,' she reminded him.

'No. Unlike most women I know, you're strangely lacking in curiosity.'

'Not really,' she admitted. 'I just don't feel it's any of my business.'

'When I first walked into your shop and saw you,' he went on, still speaking musingly, 'the first thing that struck me was the likeness. And I thought, oh God, no, not again. There can't be two in the world like that.' For a moment, there was such pain in his voice that Briony looked wonderingly at him. 'Those enormous blue eyes, the red curls, same shaped face. But there, thank God, I'm beginning to believe, the resemblance ends.'

'I remind you of someone?' It wasn't hard to deduce. 'Who?'

'My wife, my ex-wife. Charlene. But perhaps you didn't know I'd been married?' And, as Briony nodded an affirmative, he went on, 'It was Charlene I referred to when I said Matthew had a penchant for redheads. To put it bluntly, Matthew Rawlinson had an affair with my wife.' Briony gasped; whatever revelations she'd expected, it hadn't been that. 'And I have a strong suspicion,' Teale went on grimly, 'that he's the father of the child she bore. Which is why I didn't contend custody after the divorce.' He seemed to be waiting for some kind of comment.

'If that's true, I can understand you disliking Matthew,' she admitted. 'What I can't understand, after meeting Rhoda, is why Matthew should *want* to look elsewhere.'

'Oh, there's no accounting for male impulses!' He said it irritably, almost as though he applied the remark to himself as well. He seemed suddenly restless. Abruptly, he got up from his lounging position and went into the kitchen, ostensibly to check the percolator.

'I'm sorry!' Briony exclaimed. 'I'd forgotten all about the coffee.' In her haste to remedy her deficiencies as a hostess, she entered the kitchen a little too precipitately, tripped on one of Promilla's hand-tufted rugs and cannoned into Teale. Only his fast reactions saved her from a nasty fall.

She was caught up in an iron-hard embrace. Her cheek had come to rest against his chest, and she could feel the warmth of life beating beneath the soft silk of his shirt. Her nostrils inhaled the clean, tantalising male scent of him, a powerful sexual stimulant. Her idiotic heart was thumping wildly. Before she could prevent it, her body softened against the hardness of his and she felt his swift indrawn breath.

'Do you usually throw yourself into men's arms like this?' The words were light, but the tone belied them. He sounded almost annoyed. As he set her on an even keel once more and released her, Briony had the painful sensation of something being torn away from her. But Teale seemed unmoved as he turned his attention to the coffee.

Her whole body was trembling with barely concealed emotion and her mouth had gone peculiarly dry. She was mortified by her own lack of control, but even more by his apparent indifference to her. Most men would have been only too ready to take advantage of the incident. Briony had no false modesty; she knew she was not unattractive. She knew, too, that she would not have objected if he'd kissed her. Teale must have sensed that. Perhaps he thought she'd deliberately engineered the situation. Sudden swift pride provided the much needed charge of adrenalin which took her back into the sitting-room and enabled her to face him with apparent poise. She was proud to note that the hand with which she accepted the cup of coffee from him was perfectly steady.

There was an uncomfortable silence. Teale seemed to have nothing more to say and Briony couldn't think of any way to break across the tension, so she was not surprised when Teale drank his coffee in several quick gulps and rose to take his leave.

'I'll let you know what happens about the paintings. And I hope everything's straight between *us* now?' he said as she accompanied him to the shop door, which also did duty as a front door.

'Quite straight,' she said drily. She'd discovered a few new facts tonight—among them, one particularly unpalatable discovery which had opened up a range and depth of emotion she had never imagined. Teale had clarified his relationship with Matthew. But he had also made it patently clear that he was not interested in *her*. She only wished she'd been able to control that involuntary reaction to him. Teale, she thought shamefully, hadn't been able to get away fast enough!

It was only after he'd been gone for some while that she realised he'd forgotten to take the paintings.

Next morning, it took a lot of courage and a lot of urging from Promilla to make Briony drive over to Teale's house with the paintings. Her first impulse had been to put the pictures back in the studio. But, Promilla reminded her, Teale was going up to London on Monday. He might not go again for some time. Briony didn't need her friend to tell her that, for Matthew's sake, she had to make the effort, whatever the cost to her own feelings.

The coastal road was familiar this time, and it was easier to find the old manor house than it had been to find Rhoda's cottage. Cravenly, Briony admitted to herself that it would have been a relief to be able to go back and truthfully tell Promilla she'd been unsuccessful. Her friend had pooh-poohed the notion that Teale was indifferent to Briony.

'If he was, it wouldn't have mattered two hoots to him when you fell into his arms. He'd have carried it off with a joke and thought no more about it. Instead, he seems to have over-reacted. If you ask me, there's something much deeper behind him rushing off like that.'

Briony couldn't imagine what.

'Can't you? Think about it? What has your reaction been towards men over the past couple of years?'

'I've steered well clear of them.'

'Exactly. And the more attractive they were, the more you've avoided them, until now. Why? I'll tell you why,' Promilla swept on without giving Briony a chance to answer. 'It's a case of "once bitten, twice shy". And it's probably the same for Teale. It can't be very reassuring for him, either, that you're a dead ringer for his wife. Perhaps he resolved to give up women the way you once decided to give up men.'

Briony found it very difficult to believe that a man would react in the same way. Her experience of men to date was that their emotions didn't run that deep.

'Teale seems to be going to a great deal of trouble to fill you in on his personal relationships,' Promilla went on. 'Have you been as frank with him as he has with you?'

'What do you mean?' Briony prevaricated.

'You know very well. Have you told him about Jean-Luc and Iseult?'

'No. Why should I? It's none of his business.'

'It could become his business if you go on seeing him. Better to be frank now than risk leaving it too late.'

Only the thatched roof of the old manor house showed from the little private road that ran through the estate and approached the rear of the building. No other houses encroached on its privacy. There were no signs of life, other than a couple of cats lounging in the warm soil of a flowerbed. With the paintings tucked under her arm, Briony made her way round to the front door. Ancient pear trees espaliered the west wall and the grounds surrounding the manor house were a mass of colourful trees and shrubs. Among others, Briony recognised escallonia, olearia and eucalyptus. Beyond the narrow front garden, the plateau on which the house stood must have been just as nature intended it. In spring, no doubt its fine turf would be bright with wild flowers. Now the delicate tracery of ferns that edged the cliff face was already assuming bronze and gold autumnal tints. She rang the doorbell and waited tensely.

The heavy, measured tread couldn't belong to Teale. Briony's pulse-rate slowed. An elderly woman opened the door and looked at her in badly concealed surprise. Briony found herself resenting her apparent resemblance to Teale's former wife.

'Is Mr Munro in?'

'Who wants to know?' It wasn't rudely said, merely with an economy of language, as if the woman were unused to conversation.

'I'm from the Blue Unicorn in Gwinvercombe. I've brought over some paintings Mr Munro wanted. Perhaps,' she said with a sudden sense of reprieve, '*you'd* see he gets them.' The reprieve was short-lived.

'He doesn't encourage visitors when he's working. But happen you'll find him in the old barn.'

Somewhat apprehensively, Briony took the direction in which the elderly woman had pointed. Teale might be annoyed at her uninvited arrival.

There were three barns, in actual fact, hidden from the house by a handsome copse of pines and approached by a shingle path which crunched noisily beneath her high heels. She'd taken a notion, and she didn't pretend not to know why, to wear the most attractive of her outfits. The black skirt moulded her slim waist and hips then flared out in graceful lines to a full hemline. Tucked into the waistband, a softly frilled white blouse hinted at soft feminine curves beneath. To complete the outfit, she carried the matching jacket to the skirt, in case she felt cool later. At the moment, she felt far from cool.

The warmth of anticipation flushed her small, delicate face and apprehension caused a flutter beneath the frivolous frills.

From an open door in the side of the building there emerged what seemed to the startled Briony to be a vast pack of dogs. In fact, there were only three. A massive black Alsatian and a somewhat sinister-looking Dobermann made purposefully towards her, followed by a clumsily galloping, stout Springer spaniel. Briony stopped in her tracks. She wasn't generally nervous of dogs; she liked all animals. But these three might well consider her to be an unwelcome intruder.

'They won't hurt you! Heel, Max! Pincher! Sit, Sally! Remember your condition, you old fool!' Briony saw now that the brown and white Springer spaniel was heavy with pups. Teale, framed in the barn's enormous doorway, was a casually elegant figure, though simply clad in jeans and a loose chunky sweater which accentuated his masculinity. 'I see you've brought the paintings. I'm sorry you've been put to the trouble, but I'm grateful. I didn't realise I'd left the damned things behind till I was half-way home. Can't think how I came to forget them.' Briony could. He made no attempt to take them from her and Briony regarded him a little helplessly. Where did they go from here? 'You'd better come inside,' he said, as if he'd read her thoughts. 'After dragging you out here, the least I can do is repay your hospitality.'

'Really, it isn't necessary,' she protested. 'I ought to be getting back.'

'The shop doesn't open on Sundays?'

'No, but your . . . the lady who opened the door said you were busy.'

'Mrs Barrett. My housekeeper. Yes, I *was* busy. But now the mood's broken I shan't recapture it today.' Briony wasn't sure if that was meant as a reproach or not. Teale turned on his heel and led the way inside, and perforce, she had to follow him.

Outside, the buildings appeared to be conventional barns and she was totally unprepared for the interior. The lower part housed the Rolls-Royce. But then an open-tread staircase led to an upper floor. The barns had been knocked into one enormous workspace, an office. But, despite modern accessories—the chrome shelving systems, two studded steel sofas and a tubular steel and wire glass table—the origins of the place were still much in evidence.

'I wanted the place to be strictly functional, yet to retain the natural materials,' Teale said, watching her expression as she looked about her. 'The original beams are still there. I simply plastered and painted the walls.'

'And this is where you work?'

'Most of the time. You could call this my rural headquarters. I have a place in London, too. But this is my real home. Having one's office at home has good and bad points. In theory, one should be able to come in early and stay late without wrecking one's domestic life. Only it didn't work out that way!' he concluded ironically.

Briony moved around the vast area, unaware that she still clutched the paintings to her, her passport to Teale's home environment and her shield. Some of the chrome shelves were filled with colour-coded files, and on the desk was a powerful word processor and two telephones.

'One's an outside line. The other connects with the house. Mrs Barrett rang to say you were on your way over.'

The purely functional workroom was almost bleak. There were no pictures or ornaments to distract the eye. The only feature of interest was another range of shelves which held row upon row of books. She studied them with interest. It had always been her contention that you could tell a lot about someone's character from their reading taste.

Many were reference books. Among others, there was a handsomely bound set of encyclopaedia, a fat well-used dictionary, a *Roget's Thesaurus* and a well-thumbed *Writers' and Artists' Yearbook*. Evidently he was a writer of some kind. Her gaze moved onwards over a row of books, all uniform in size. Their gaudy dustcovers seemed familiar, and without asking permission she took one down. The design on the front showed a staring, fear-distorted face.

'*Day of the Goliath* by David Astra,' she read aloud. She turned to look at Teale, suddenly aware of a tangible, alert silence. '*You're* David Astra?' she asked doubtfully. It was only a couple of weeks since she'd read one of Astra's sophisticated horror stories. She had a taste for spine-chillers, and currently he was her favourite author.

Teale inclined his head, an odd expression on his face.

'Guilty! But don't feel you have to be polite and say you like them.'

'But I *do*! At least, I find them compulsive reading. They fascinate me and they frighten me at the same time.' His books exploited the full extent of human fears. Sometimes, they also included very explicit sexual scenes. Briony felt her cheeks colouring as she remembered just how graphic some of those scenes were. Yet, reading them, she had never been aware of distaste, rather of an erotic, pulsating excitement. Very similar, she realised, to the way Teale himself affected her.

Having read so many of his books, it was a strange but interesting experience to meet the author face to face, and difficult to reconcile the author's persona with that of Teale Munro. David Astra's unfailing ability to produce bestsellers had placed him among the handful of men to whom others turned time and time again for a sure-fire hit. Publishers paid him huge advances before he even knew what his next book would be about. But as far as possible he had always shunned publicity. His likeness never appeared on the jackets of his books and so far he had managed to discourage interviewers. Releases via the press media were often the product of mere speculation. He had no agent, preferring to deal directly with his publishers, and he had resisted all attempts to turn his books into film scripts.

'Now I know why you're always so busy. I suppose you're constantly working to deadlines?'

'Not only that. Once I begin a story, I work on it every day. If I don't, I risk it going stale on me and getting the dreaded writers' block. Look,' he went on, 'since I've finished work for the day, why don't we go over to the house for that coffee? I think you may find the surroundings more to your taste.'

'If you're sure...?' She wanted to stay, but wasn't sure she should.

'Let me take those from you first. They'll be quite safe from prying eyes up here.' He moved to take the pictures which she'd forgotten she still clutched and, as he did so, his hand inadvertently brushed against the soft swell of her breast and Briony knew her nipples had sprung into agonising, independent life. She swallowed and shivered, closing her eyes briefly against a sensation that was almost faintness.

'Briony? Are you all right?' His voice was harsh and at once she pulled herself together.

'Fine.' She summoned up a little laugh. 'Just a goose walking over my grave! Perhaps I've been reading too many of your horror stories,' she quipped.

'Mmmn. Maybe.' Teale sounded unconvinced and his gaze on her was still speculative.

She was careful to keep an arm's length between them as they walked side by side back to the house. On the way, she noticed several more cats curled in sleepy corners.

They entered the house by the rear door, through a vast kitchen equipped with every sparkling modernity known to man, then through a baize door into the contrasting grace and charm of a past age.

Muted corals, browns, subdued greens and rich ochres dominated the colour scheme, setting off the rich wood of antique furniture. In the sitting-room, rich red walls and golden ochre ceilings were a foil for dark oak and tapestry upholstery. One complete wall was filled with books, not Teale's work this time, but the classics and modern greats. Briony recognised several titles by P D James, another of her favourites. A white marble fireplace held a set piece of objects displayed in the Victorian fashion—a marble clock, a handsomely bound book, a candlestick and a mediaeval print. Briony exclaimed with delight over a harmonium, a typical Victorian musical instrument, set in one corner.

'I've always wanted to be able to afford one of these. But they always fetch such a high price at auctions.'

'You go to auction sales?' He rang a bell, presumably to summon the housekeeper.

'Not as often as I'd like to. Promilla and I take it in turns, when we can be spared from the shop. We're both keen on Victoriana.'

'One of my own passions.'

'You have a lovely home,' Briony said enviously. 'It really lends itself to antiques. I'm afraid our bits and pieces are sadly cramped. It's almost got to the stage where I daren't buy any more.'

'No prospects of expansion?'

'Not at present.'

A silver tea service and wafer-thin sandwiches were brought in by Mrs Barrett and placed on a long sofa table. After the housekeeper had gone, Briony asked

Teale about his writing. She was genuinely interested, but she also had to keep her mind on intellectual subjects. It would be all too easy to let herself dwell on other more disturbing topics, such as the vital way his hair sprang back from a widow's peak, and the way it curled slightly at his collar. She knew an insidious desire to plunge her hands into its dark luxuriance.

'Did you always want to be a writer?' As far back as Briony could remember, she'd always wanted to paint.

'Not in the sense that I'm a writer now.' He waved her to a seat on the sofa, then stood, one arm resting negligently on the mantelpiece. Another gesture of his long, lean hand invited Briony to pour the tea. 'I started out as a TV journalist, worked my way up and eventually graduated to my own chat show.'

'But you're not on television now.' If that had been the case, she would have recognised him. 'Milk? Sugar?' Though she was glad of something to do, Briony was afraid he might notice that her hands were slightly unsteady.

'I chucked television about eight years ago. I wanted to find out if I *could* write.' He grinned wryly. 'I'm still not sure I can.' And, as she made a noise of polite protest, 'Be honest. Are you ever totally satisfied with *your* work?' She shook her head. 'My friends and family thought I was mad, of course. Charlene, especially. I was in television when we met. She was a continuity girl. We'd only been married a year. But she liked the glamour that went with being married to a television personality.' His irregular features twisted for a moment. 'Come to think of it, that's probably why she accepted me in the first place.'

'Wasn't there as much kudos in being married to a famous writer?' Briony handed him his tea, careful as she did so that their hands should not brush.

'Ah, but I wasn't famous then. There was a lot of hard slog ahead of me. That was something else Charlene didn't understand, that a lot of people still don't understand.' As he took the tea, he moved to sit beside her on the sofa, and Briony felt the muscles of her stomach tense. 'Of necessity, writing is a very solitary occupation. You have to be selfish. You have to shut other people out of your life to a great extent.' Had he shut his wife out? Was that what Matthew had meant when he had said Teale didn't need women? 'Charlene thought this place was the back of beyond. She didn't see why I couldn't write just as well in London. That's partly why I kept the flat on, so she could get up to town now and then.'

'It must have been a hard decision for you to make— to give up all the fame and a safe career for the uncertainty of being self-employed, to become an anonymous figure again.'

He shook his head and leant back, crossing his legs. The movement brought him closer, but Briony dared not edge away. Instead, she had to suffer the brush of his arm against hers as he gestured to emphasise his words.

'The only consideration was the financial one. All fame is transitory anyway, and being a television personality is unreal. Let's face it, if you appear on the small screen often enough you're bound to be well known, whether it's deserved or not. But if you disappear for a few months you're forgotten. Books at least endure.'

'And do you write *all* the time?' Briony had always thought it would be marvellous to be able to paint without interruption, until she'd experienced the reality. Lonely for the first time in her life, she'd found ideas did not breed in a vacuum. She needed the stimulation of life, found that it was necessary to have people around her some of the time.

'Pretty well. It's a strange phenomenon. When I'm in the middle of a book, I think I'll be glad to get the darned thing finished. But as soon as it is I can't wait to start another.'

'Painting's a bit like that,' Briony agreed. 'That can be a lonely pastime, too. I don't like anyone talking to me when I'm actually working.'

'In that case, you'll probably understand when I say I would never have got married if I'd known what I know now.'

Briony experienced an acute depression of spirits. It was foolish. Teale Munro had given her no excuse at all to expect any deepening of their acquaintance. But she had hoped. And, although she knew it was probably unwise, she wasn't quite ready to give up that faint hope.

'But don't you ever get . . . lonely?' That was as close as Briony dared to go in asking about his personal needs, but Teale had fewer inhibitions.

'What you mean is, do I ever *need* a woman, physically?' His bluntness made her blush. 'Yes, I do.'

'*Matthew* said you didn't,' she blurted out, then cursed her own frankness.

'Possibly my needs and Matthew's are rather different,' he said drily. 'But I don't think he was referring to the physical. I have the same needs and desires as any man. And the same temptations to break my own rules,' he said thoughtfully. For a long time, he held her eyes with his own and Briony quivered under their assessment, wishing that, just once, he might find himself tempted to kiss her. 'But, if he meant that I don't need a constant stream of women to bolster up my ego, then he's right. Perhaps if Matthew could overcome his sense of his own unworthiness he might be less dependent on women and their emotional support.'

'In my book, that doesn't make him weak,' Briony argued. 'It makes him rather admirable. The relationship between men and women shouldn't be purely sexual. There *should* be emotional and spiritual ties.'

'Then I confess I've never experienced them. I suppose that lowers me in your estimation?'

'Actually, it makes me feel rather sorry for you.' In a low, husky voice, Briony added, 'I think it must be rather dreadful not to know how it feels to be in love.'

'Ah, love!' Teale said cynically. 'A typically female description of the sensation. I prefer to call it "need". But it's surprising how you can sublimate such "needs" in work. And it isn't fair to ask any woman to share the kind of life I lead. I realised that long ago. Charlene used to complain that even when I was with her my mind was elsewhere. It was true. I'd be smitten by an idea and have to get it down there and then. And if she spoke to me in the middle of a sentence and destroyed my train of thought I knew I'd never recapture it in exactly the same form. And I'd be furious. A writer is impossible to live with.'

Briony wondered if she was imagining it, or whether he was deliberately making such a strong case, warning her off, in effect. Perhaps it was time to steer the conversation into less personal channels. She stood up and moved to the window which overlooked the barren coastline.

'You certainly have the isolation here that you need for your work.'

It was a bad move, for he came to stand beside her, closer than if she'd remained seated.

'Yes. And because of it I've also succeeded in retaining my anonymity. I'd be obliged if you didn't let it be known in Gwinvercombe who I am. I've no wish to be lionised. That's why I never invite anyone to visit me here.' At his words, Briony flushed painfully.

'I'm sorry,' she said stiffly. 'Why didn't you tell me straight away that I was intruding?'

'Good heavens!' he exclaimed. 'That *was* clumsy of me.' He put a hand on her arm. 'My dear Briony, I wasn't implying... It was very good of you to remedy my forgetfulness. What I meant was that I had my fill of opening church fêtes and being pursued by predatory women in my TV days.' His tone became cynical. 'There's no other aphrodisiac quite as potent as fame.'

Briony wasn't so sure. It certainly wasn't the knowledge of who he was that was affecting *her* in this way, so that her body clamoured to be nearer to him. She half wished he would remove his hand, half hoped he wouldn't. She tried to pass the moment off lightly.

'You mean, they didn't fancy you just for yourself?' Had she allowed a note of incredulity to enter her voice? He was certainly looking down at her rather strangely.

'You find that surprising?'

'Frankly, yes.' She tried to make it sound purely academic. 'I've met one or two famous men who were also extremely unattractive. I certainly didn't find their notoriety prompted me to overlook their total lack of charisma.'

'It would be interesting to know,' he murmured reflectively, 'just where *I* come on your scale of values.' If that was meant flirtatiously, he'd left it a little late. His message had come through strong and clear: no involvement for Teale Munro.

'I've never really thought about it.' It was a good excuse to step a little away from him, and escape the warm hand whose touch seemed to penetrate the flimsy material of her blouse as though it were non-existent. But now she had to carry it through and pretend to appraise him, a task which made it difficult to retain her assumed poise and air of detachment.

She already knew every detail of his appearance by heart. The face, long, lean and hawkish with its clean-cut jawline. Unwisely, perhaps, she found herself concentrating on the mouth. Its full bottom lip had more than a hint of passion, the narrow upper spoke of impatience. As she looked, it twisted into that one-sided, half-sardonic, half-humorous smile. Grey eyes, gleaming like molten silver, met hers stare for stare.

'Well?' he invited.

'Well enough.' She nodded casual approval. 'Not my type of course, but...'

'*Not* your type, eh?' He seemed disproportionately amused. 'Is that the truth, I wonder, or some kind of challenge?'

'It's certainly not a challenge,' she retorted promptly. She congratulated herself on having evaded the issue rather neatly. 'I'm not in the market for a flirtation, any more than you are. Like you, I'm very busy, too busy for involvements even if I felt any inclination that way.' Until recently, that had been the truth. She looked at her watch and affected astonishment. 'Goodness! I really mustn't take up any more of your time.'

'Oh, but surely you can spare a little longer?' His regret *sounded* genuine. 'I thought you might like to see the rest of the house. It's very old and absolutely unique in these parts. In fact,' he seemed quite struck by the thought, 'perhaps you might like to paint it? Do you accept commissions?'

'If the subject interests me.' Right now, she'd like to paint his portrait, she thought. It would give her an excuse for more open study of his dark, lean, vital face.

'And would this house interest you?'

'It might.' It would be an excuse to come here again, perhaps several times.

'Then let me show you over it,' he coaxed, his hand on her arm once more.

'I don't need to see the interior to paint the exterior view,' she pointed out.

'You paint portraits, full-length figures?' And, as she nodded, a little bewildered by this apparent change of tack, Teale asked, 'For that, you had to study anatomy, right?' Again she nodded. 'Then I don't see the difference. I want you to know about the anatomy of my house before you paint it. I want you to absorb the atmosphere.'

It made a kind of sense. The only trouble, Briony thought, was that she was particularly sensitive to atmosphere. She already liked what she'd seen of this gracious old house. Suppose she were to fall in love with it irrevocably as she'd... Oh, God! The trend of her own thoughts, the realisation they brought, appalled her...as irrevocably as she'd fallen in love with its owner, and with less encouragement. In fact, no encouragement at all. Her sense of shock must have shown in her face.

'What on earth have I said to make you look like that?'

'Nothing,' she denied hastily. 'It's just that I don't see how I can find time to accept a commission just now. It would mean being away from the shop. And soon I'll have students to consider, too.'

'The shop isn't open on Sundays. Do you take students on Sundays?'

'No, but,' indignantly, 'I have to rest some time.'

'What could be more relaxing,' he coaxed, 'than doing something you enjoy? And I'm not a slave-driver. You could work as many or as few hours as you liked, with lunch and an evening meal thrown in, if you like. And,' he added as though this were the clinching incentive, 'I'd keep right out of your way. You need not see me at all if you don't want to. Though I hope you *will* give me your company now and again.'

He seemed to have completely changed his tune, Briony thought, not without suspicion. From total discouragement, he now seemed to be positively encouraging her to visit his home. And she was tempted. But she was also doubtful about his motives. He wasn't in love with her. Why else should he crave her society?

'I'll think about it,' she temporised.

'Then you'll let me show you round before you go?'

The old house held many secrets. No two rooms were on the same level. Passages led here and there, coming to sudden dead ends. The gleaming floors and stair-treads groaned their age.

'It's enormous,' Briony exclaimed when finally they reached the top floor. She couldn't help reflecting what a marvellous studio the attics would make. And the things that could be done with the house's many rooms! All her creative instincts were stimulated.

'It was meant to be a family home, of course,' Teale said. 'And that's why I bought it in the first place. My parents were still alive then. They lived here for a short while. And then, of course, I'd hoped for children, several of them.'

'You like children?' Briony asked him.

'Very much. I'm extremely fond of Rhoda's children. Since I'm unlikely to have any family of my own now, this house and everything else I own will be theirs some day.' He was thoughtful for a moment, then mused aloud, 'I enjoy writing for its own sake. But the wealth it brings is a responsibility. Do you think it corrupts the young to have money left to them which they haven't earned?'

'I've no idea. But it's a consideration that's not likely to worry me,' Briony said drily. 'I suppose it's due to the increasing amount of leisure time, but artists seem to be a glut on the market nowadays. You'd have to be really exceptional to make a living solely by painting. I make only a modest income, hence the shop. But, Teale, you do have a child,' she remembered.

'That,' he was grim again, 'is a debatable point. At least I'm certain Rhoda's children have *some* Munro blood. I can't speak with any certainty about Scott.'

'But that's not the kiddie's fault!'

'No,' he agreed. 'And I know it may seem peculiarly old-fashioned of me in this day and age, but our parents brought Rhoda and me up to have certain values. I was faithful to my marriage vows and I expected total fidelity from my wife. I have strong views on any kind of promiscuity.'

In principle, she agreed with him. But was he totally intolerant, making no allowances even for youthful ignorance and folly? She was glad she'd remained fixed in her determination not to tell Teale about the one lapse in *her* life.

CHAPTER FIVE

'You should have told him there and then,' Promilla said sagely. 'If he *is* as inflexible as that, at least you'd know now where you stand. Though somehow I can't believe he'd be so totally lacking in compassion as to condemn you for a teenage peccadillo. But, if he is, then you're better off without him.'

'I'm not even *with* him,' Briony retorted with feeling. 'That's why it would seem presumptuous to start telling him my life history, as if it could be of any possible interest to him.' Briony sighed, then went on, 'It's probably stupid of me to go on hoping there'll ever be anything between us. But I didn't want to completely burn my boats where he's concerned. And if I'd told him...' She shrugged and smiled a little wryly. 'At least he paid me a compliment—a rather back-handed one. He said that, apart from his sister, it wasn't often he met a woman with whom he could hold an intelligent conversation. That, perhaps because in our different ways we were both exponents of the arts, we had a lot in common.'

'Well, that's *something*! Keep working on that side of your relationship and maybe the rest will follow naturally,' Promilla encouraged.

Briony hugged her friend.

'What would I do without you, Prom? You're such a comfort to me.'

Thank God she'd always been able to confide in Promilla, Briony thought that night as she got ready for bed. She didn't know where she'd be now without the other woman's friendship and advice. Promilla was the only person now who knew about Briony's 'teenage peccadillo', as she'd called it.

His name was Jean-Luc. He'd been an art student in the same year as Briony. With his blond good looks and attractive accent, he had a glamour none of the other young men of her age possessed. Briony swiftly became infatuated, and she knew her girlfriends envied her the young Frenchman's assiduous attentions.

She took Jean-Luc home during the holidays. But, despite the doubts expressed by her widower father about the young man's suitability, his warnings went unheeded. Fathers, she knew, were often stuffy about their daughters' boyfriends.

Educated at a convent a few miles away from her home, Briony had had a strict upbringing and she'd revelled in the free and easy life of art college, of London, and her social life, the unending stream of parties.

Though he hadn't been keen on her becoming an art student, Briony's father had made her a generous allowance, and most of the friends with whom she associated were similarly situated. Thus drink flowed freely at the parties she attended. Some students, she knew, also experimented with drugs. She wasn't that foolish, but she *had* got tipsy once or twice. It was on one of these occasions that she and Jean-Luc made love and she conceived.

Of all her friends, Jean-Luc was the least affluent, but reluctantly he agreed to marry her. His parents, he'd admitted, would be shocked by any other course of action. By this, she assumed he meant abortion; but the idea of such a thing never even crossed her mind.

They went together to see her father. Briony had known John Kent would be distressed by her irresponsible behaviour, but it had never occurred to her not to confide in him. Her mother had died when Briony was a baby, and though she and her father had never been very close he was the only person to whom she could go in her extremity. John Kent had had long conversations, with her and with Jean-Luc. And Briony was bitterly hurt and incredulous when she discovered what her father had done. He'd offered Jean-Luc money *not* to marry her. Worse, Jean-Luc had accepted. He hadn't loved her as she loved him. This realisation tempered her reproaches to her father, and John Kent indicated his willingness to support both her and the baby.

'It's folly to rush into things just because a baby's on the way,' her father had told her. 'It's the worst possible basis for marriage. You're both far too young. I don't want to see my only daughter ruin her whole life.'

John kept his word and he welcomed the little girl, so like Briony in appearance. He grew very fond of his granddaughter, and in this mutual affection Briony felt closer to him than ever before.

When Iseult was six, Briony met Bob Daish, younger son of a family who had just moved into the neighbouring farm, and thought herself in love again. Bob asked her to marry him and declared himself willing to accept Iseult.

They were within a few weeks of their wedding when disaster struck. John Kent suffered a sudden massive heart attack, from which he never recovered. After the funeral, there was another blow. Unwise investments had left Briony's father almost penniless, his home heavily mortgaged. Everything had to be sold up to pay off his debts. Despite John's assurances to her, there was nothing left over for Briony and her daughter.

It was a week or two before it struck Briony that Bob's manner towards her had altered. But when, finally, she taxed him with it, he admitted he no longer wished to marry her. A conversation which became acrimonious revealed that, not being his father's heir, he had been relying on Briony inheriting her father's house and farm.

With no family, no money and no home, Briony turned to the only other person she could rely on to help her, Promilla Kadri, with whom she'd always kept in touch.

Promilla was only too willing to give the shattered Briony refuge. But Briony knew it could only be temporary. She couldn't impose on her friend's kindness indefinitely. Hoping to use her artistic talents, she tried to find work.

Eventually, as luck would have it, her search took her to the London branch of an advertising agency which turned out to be owned by Jean-Luc. Now a successful businessman, he commuted between Paris and London.

On the day of Briony's interview he was in London. He recognised her at once. She didn't get the job, but when the interviews were over Jean-Luc took her on one side and asked her to remain behind.

Unsuspectingly, she answered his probing questions about her personal life and circumstances. Too late, she realised his interest was not in her, but in his daughter. Jean-Luc, she discovered, was married, but his wife was delicate and there were no children. His proposition stunned Briony.

'The money your father settled on me helped me to go into advertising. Let me have my daughter and I'll give you the capital you need to set yourself up in some kind of business.'

She refused, of course. She adored Iseult, and there was no way she was going to part with her if she could help it. But Jean-Luc was nothing if not persistent. He visited her at Promilla's flat. He bombarded her with letters and telephone calls, sent presents for Iseult. He pointed out that Briony could barely support the child, but that with her father Iseult would have boundless advantages. He was charming with Iseult and before long the child adored him and looked forward to his visits. Finally worn down by despair, her inability to find work, her fast dwindling resources and the conviction that she was acting in Iseult's best interests, Briony capitulated. Her only stipulation was that she must be allowed contact with her daughter, and to this Jean-Luc agreed.

Iseult was only seven when Jean-Luc took her back to Paris. The child would soon settle down, he assured a tearful Briony. He would, he promised, bring Iseult to England twice a year and allow her to visit her natural mother.

That was over two years ago. To do him justice, Jean-Luc had kept his word. He'd given Briony the lump sum that had enabled her to go into partnership with Promilla here in Gwinvercombe. She'd missed Iseult dreadfully, of course. But she saw her twice a year, the child wrote regularly and Briony had learned to sink her unhappiness in hard work. Fortunately, Iseult had taken to Jean-Luc's frail wife, who treated the little girl as indulgently as if she'd been her own.

So, at first, Iseult had been content enough. But she was growing up and lately her letters had contained worrying hints that all was not well at home. She told Briony of constant rows between Jean-Luc and his wife. Iseult was a mature ten-year-old now and, reading between the lines, Briony guessed Jean-Luc was seeing other women. If the child was allowed to visit her at Christmas, she would be able to find out if Iseult was really unhappy.

When Briony pulled up the shop blinds next morning and began to renew the window display, she saw the silver-grey Rolls-Royce glide slowly past. Her heart somersaulted. But then she remembered; Teale was on his way to London. It was less hassle, he said, to go by train. He must have kept his promise to lend his sister the car.

Sure enough, it was Rhoda who entered the shop a few minutes later. A little breathlessly she enquired, 'Not late, am I?'

'No. We're up early for once. Prom's in the studio, laying out some work for you.'

'That's a very satisfying sound,' Promilla said later that morning. Her dark head tilted on one side, she was listening to the steady hum of the sewing machine. Although much of the finer detail of her craftwork was done by hand, the machine also had its part to play. 'I've never seen a woman work so fast. At this rate,' she said half-jokingly, 'I may be able to take time off to go to Karachi, after all.'

'I don't see why you shouldn't.' Briony was perfectly serious. 'You haven't had a holiday in two years. And it's not that you can't afford it.' Promilla's parents had left her comfortably off.

It was obvious from the start that Rhoda was going to fit in well, and both girls liked her immensely. Matthew didn't seem to object to his wife working practically alongside him. In fact, he remarked once that it was quite like the old days, when they'd been going through their 'self-sufficiency' period.

'We still are in a way,' Rhoda pointed out. 'We grow our own vegetables, we have the nanny-goats for milk and the chickens for eggs.' Briony suspected that most of the industry was Rhoda's. Matthew was totally impractical. She was full of admiration, too, for the way the other woman had coped during her husband's prolonged absence.

Teale had been away for nearly two weeks before Briony nerved herself to enquire about him from Rhoda. His sister, of course, knew nothing of his errand to the art gallery. Over their morning coffee she told Briony, 'All I know is that he intended to see his publishers about a jacket for his latest book. Being one of their top authors, he has a large say in the design. He was only supposed to be gone a day or two. But then he phoned me last Thursday to say Charlene's mother had contacted him. Charlene wanted to see him urgently.'

'Oh?' It was difficult to show only polite interest when she was avid for further information.

'Yes. I don't know why.' Rhoda looked worried. 'I hope she's not trying to get him back after all this time.' So did Briony!

'Is that likely?' Briony hoped she didn't sound as aghast as she felt. 'How long have they been divorced?'

'Let's see. Little Scott must be six now. So it must be five and a half years. No, it's not likely.' Rhoda was obviously reassuring herself as much as answering the question. But Briony felt a little easier in her own mind. Of anyone, his twin sister must know Teale best.

'I suppose you've heard all the gossip?' Rhoda asked as she took up her sewing again. 'Why Teale divorced Charlene?' She didn't wait for a reply but went on. 'She *was* playing around. I don't know who with. But I do know *Matthew* wasn't having an affair with her. Teale wouldn't believe that, but *I know*. And I told him so at the time. Did he really think I wouldn't know if my own husband was being unfaithful to me?'

'Then why did Matthew go away? It *was* about the same time that Charlene left, wasn't it?'

'The same day, unfortunately. But that was coincidence.' She looked challengingly at Briony.

'I'm not saying *I* don't believe you,' Briony said hastily. 'I want to believe you. I like Matthew and I like you. I'd like to see Matthew succeed with his painting.' She put down her empty cup and walked over to the easel where his latest work was in progress and studied it as they spoke.

'It would be the making of him,' Rhoda agreed. 'He should never have given it up all those years ago. But my family brought pressure to bear on him; he thought he was conforming for my sake, trying to hold down a conventional job. But I didn't care about that. As long as I had Matt and the children I was happy. We would have managed. As it was, he went from job to job, getting more and more discouraged and finally thoroughly depressed.'

'Has he always been so moody?' Briony remembered how Matthew had been when he'd first come to the Blue Unicorn and thought she could see an improvement in him.

'He's always been highly strung, ever since I've known him. He veers from extreme highs to extreme lows. But I know how to calm him down and how to cheer him up. If he'd been happy in his work, I'm sure maturity would have solved all that. I think Teale's accusation was the last straw. Charlene didn't deny it. And suddenly one day Matthew disappeared and that was the last I saw of him for six years, until a few weeks ago. Six years, Briony!' Rhoda's voice shook at the remembrance. 'Can you imagine what it was like? Not knowing where he was, or even if he was still alive?'

'Did you go to the police?'

'We tried everything.' Rhoda stood up and began to pace the studio as if she was reliving those years of anxiety, of waiting for news. 'But he seemed to have disappeared without a trace. Charlene swore she didn't know where he was. We kept getting reports that he'd been seen, first in one place, then in another, all over the country. I followed up every lead. Nothing. Finally, Teale forbade me to go haring off on these wild-goose chases. The disappointment when I found another dead end was destroying me.'

'And then he turned up here, practically on his own doorstep.'

'When I heard he'd been seen here in Gwinvercombe, I thought it was just another unfounded rumour. Teale was away. He had the car, in any case. And Libby—that's my youngest—was down with chicken-pox. But I couldn't let it go, just in case. So I phoned Teale in London.'

'And he came chasing home, and that's when I had my first encounter with him,' Briony said wryly.

'Yes.' Rhoda's face expressed concern. 'He told me about that. I'm sorry you were on the receiving end of his anger. But I never believed for a moment that there was anything between you and Matthew. And I rather suspect Teale's glad there wasn't. He has a great deal of respect for you, Briony.' She sat down again at her machine, but she did not begin work immediately. Instead, her grey eyes, so like her brother's, were fixed consideringly on Briony's face. 'I wish...'

'Did you ever find out where Matthew had been all those years?' Briony interrupted quickly. She thought she knew what Rhoda wished, but she was afraid to hear her say it, in case she betrayed herself.

'Yes.' Rhoda hesitated, then asked 'Can I trust you, Briony? This is something I haven't even told Teale.'

'If you'd rather not...'

'Actually, it will be a relief in a way to tell someone. I had a job to get it out of Matthew. He was so mortified.'

'It won't go any further, I promise.'

'He left here determined to get some kind of job. He wasn't going to come back until he had something to show for it, and he did work for a while. But then he had a complete nervous breakdown. He was in a psychiatric hospital for four years under a different name. He didn't want any of his friends or family to know. As he began to improve, they sent him to rehabilitation classes. Part of the therapy was painting, and Matthew began to rediscover himself. Have you never wondered why he doesn't come here on Mondays?' And, as Briony nodded, Rhoda explained, 'He has to go for regular check-ups.' Rhoda stood up and came to join Briony at the easel. She looked critically at the landscape Briony was studying. 'If he *could* make a success of this, I really believe there'd be no looking back. Already his style is calmer, more self-controlled.'

'Wasn't it rather strange that he should be living round here,' Briony said, 'and coming to me for painting and yet you didn't know he was home?'

'Poor Matt!' Rhoda sighed. 'He wasn't sure what kind of reception he'd get after six years, especially since I'd moved out of our old house in Barnstaple and into Teale's cottage. And yet the poor lamb so wanted to be near us.'

'You must love him very much to be so understanding. It can't have been easy, waiting for him all those years. And he loves you,' Briony said wistfully. 'It must be rather wonderful to love each other like that.'

'Yes. That's what Teale has never been able to understand—why Matthew and I are so good for each other. I don't think Teale's ever known what it's like to be really in love. I certainly don't believe he was ever in love with Charlene. I don't know what he'd do if he ever fell for someone really hard.' She chuckled ruefully. 'I think it might upset his pride.'

'What did *you* think of Charlene?'

'She was pretty. A little like you to look at, but much more superficial. She hadn't your depth of character, or your intelligence. All she was interested in was her appearance and having a good time. D'you know, Briony,

I've known her actually change her outfit four times in one day. She even kept a chart so she didn't repeat the combination that week! As for having a good time, that meant going to parties, preferably where celebrities gathered. When she found Teale couldn't be dragged back to that brittle, insincere life-style, she started going on her own. I know she was running around with other men. But I can't say for sure whether she was actually physically unfaithful to Teale.'

'What about little Scott? Do *you* think he's Teale's child?'

'Yes. And anyone who saw him would say the same. But Teale either can't or won't see it.'

'Teale came home last night,' Rhoda reported on Saturday morning. 'I gave his housekeeper a lift into town. She said he's brought little Scott with him. I'm dying to know why.' So was Briony.

'Simple,' Promilla said, when Briony told her. 'Go up tomorrow and find out.'

'Oh, yes, just like that?' Briony said sarcastically. 'Won't it look a bit obvious?'

'You've been up there the last two Sundays, painting,' Promilla reminded her. 'So why not tomorrow? We're well into October already. There won't be many more fine weekends for sitting out sketching.'

But Promilla wouldn't have been able to persuade her if she hadn't already wanted to go, Briony thought as she took the by now familiar route to the old manor house. She wouldn't announce her arrival to anyone, but would just take up her usual position and begin work. If Teale chose to acknowledge her presence, that was up to him.

It was difficult to concentrate on the painting, especially since it was necessary from time to time to look at her model, and Briony found herself wondering whether she *had* seen a movement at a window, or whether she had been observed.

In spite of this constant alertness, she was startled into a betraying gasp, her face, as always in strong emotion, going first pale and then fiery red, when Teale came upon her unawares.

'I'm sure you must be dying for a coffee break. You seem to have been out here since the crack of dawn.'

She *had* been early. But then, she'd been awake off and on half the night anticipating this encounter. Finally, it had seemed she might as well get up.

'I've brought a flask,' she told him, but she was pleased when he insisted she would enjoy a freshly brewed cup far better.

'How's the painting coming along?' asked Teale as they walked towards the house. The rough-mown grass was uneven and he placed a supportive hand beneath her elbow.

'I've only done the preliminary sketches so far. I like to transfer them to canvas and work them up in the studio. Our climate doesn't really lend itself to painting out of doors. Either it rains or else it's windy and you get dust and leaves stuck to the canvas.' She was speaking rapidly, nervously, as she always seemed to at any initial encounter with Teale. The feel of his hard hand on her arm wasn't helping, either. She took a deep breath and forced herself to say more calmly, 'How was your trip to London?'

'Moderately successful.' He ushered her ahead of him into the drawing-room, where someone had already set out a coffee-pot, two cups and an assortment of home-made biscuits. Teale invited her to sit down and took his place beside her. 'I'm afraid business got rather pushed to one side by family affairs, but I did have time to take Rawlinson's painting, the still life, to the gallery you suggested.'

'You mentioned my name?'

'Yes, and they'll be in touch with you. They seemed reluctant to commit themselves to me. Perhaps because they knew I was a relative.'

'You said you gave them *one* painting,' Briony realised. 'But you took two?'

'Yes. I had rather more success with that one.' He watched her closely for any reaction. 'I was discussing a jacket for my latest book and it seemed to me that the abstract fitted the bill. The publisher loved it, Rawlinson will get the credit—and substantial rights—if he agrees to its use.'

'But that's marvellous!' Briony's heart-shaped face glowed with enthusiasm. Impulsively, she put her hand on Teale's arm. 'That *was* good of you!' For a moment, she sensed a curious stillness in him, then he moved away and her hand dropped to her side. She felt curiously snubbed.

'I hope *Rawlinson* will think so,' Teale said drily. 'He may damn me for an interfering so-and-so. He might refuse to sign the agreement.'

'Not if we get Rhoda to tell him,' Briony suggested. 'She knows the right way to handle him.'

'Woman, the eternal manipulator!' It wasn't said unpleasantly, but with a certain wry amusement. 'I'm beginning to feel a little manipulated myself. If it hadn't been for you, I doubt I would have interested myself that much in Rawlinson's affairs.'

'Oh!' Briony wasn't sure if that was a compliment or not. To cover her uncertainty she looked around the room as though admiring her surroundings. But pretence became genuine. With a fire burning in the large grate to offset the chill of the early autumn day, the room seemed homely and welcoming, despite the richness and value of its contents.

'Yes.' Suddenly it was Teale who seemed ill at ease. He rose and walked to the window, staring out at the sea, which was grey and somewhat turbulent this morning. With apparent inconsequence, he said, 'I saw Charlene while I was in London.'

'Rhoda mentioned it,' Briony said when Teale seemed to have lapsed into silence once more. She waited painfully for him to go on.

'And I find I owe Matthew an apology.' She guessed he was a man who didn't find apologising easy. But Briony's spirits, which had dwindled, had risen again. He wasn't going to tell her he was reconciled with his former wife. 'He wasn't having an affair with her, though she did her best to lead him on. Just to spite me, I suspect.'

'She actually admitted that?' Briony couldn't contain her surprise.

Teale turned to face her once more.

'Charlene is a very sick woman. Cancer.' He said the word brusquely. 'She knows she may not have very long to live.' Briony searched his face for pain, but saw only natural regret for a fellow human being's mortality.

'So she wanted to clear her conscience?'

'I don't know about conscience. I don't think Charlene ever had any particular religious creed.' He moved back to the sofa and sat down. 'Her only saving grace as far as I'm concerned has been that she's always been genuinely fond of her child. No, it was a kind of trade-in. The truth in exchange for my promise to take Scott, acknowledge him as my son and bring him up.'

'You agreed, of course?'

'Subject to a blood test, yes.' And, at Briony's incredulous expression, 'Though there's nothing between me and Charlene any more, I *am* sorry for her. But I couldn't allow my common sense to be swayed by sentimentality for a dying woman, could I? There was too much at stake. I had to be sure, don't you see?' He seemed to be pleading with her for understanding.

'Yes, I do see,' she assured him. 'And . . . ?'

'He's of my blood all right.' Teale sighed. 'It's going to take some getting used to, just as it'll take me a while to get used to having a young child around the house. God knows what I'm going to do with him.'

'Get to know him, I should hope,' Briony said rather indignantly.

'Yes!' Teale ran a distracted hand through his thick, dark hair. 'Will *you* help me, Briony?' The question was totally unexpected and she floundered a little.

'How can *I* help? I'd like to, of course,' she added hastily as Teale's face seemed to express disappointment. 'But I . . .'

'Being so young, I thought he might feel more at ease with a woman—a young woman. Mrs Barrett's too old to look after a small boy. Would you object if Rhoda brought him into the shop sometimes? I don't think he'd be any trouble. He's a very quiet child.'

Briony felt a sharp stab of disappointment. For a moment, she'd believed Teale wanted her to involve herself personally in Scott's care.

'I suppose it would be all right. I'll have to ask Promilla, of course.'

'I bet she won't mind. I think your charming friend rather approves of me!' His sudden grin was infectious and, despite her chagrin, Briony found herself smiling back.

'The conceit of some people!'

'If I *were* conceited,' he said wryly, 'I'd take it for granted that you'd come out with us at weekends—with Scott and me, I mean,' he added as Briony looked questioningly at him. 'But I'm *not* taking it for granted, I'm asking. Briony, *will* you take pity on us? It would make things much easier—for both of us.'

She knew he was referring to himself and Scott. But his invitation might make things easier from *her* point of view. Teale wanted to get close to his son. She wanted to get closer to Teale.

'I'd like that very much,' she said. But she simply could not conceal the pleasure she felt and it irradiated her whole face and glowed in the blue eyes that looked up at him.

'Sunday?'

'Sunday!' she confirmed happily.

Summer was far behind them that Sunday. But the glow of September had continued into October; and there was a correspondingly warm glow in Briony's heart as she drove through the twisting lanes and along the coastline to the manor house.

She was glad she'd worn jeans and sweater and comfortable shoes, for Teale's idea of a suitable outing for his son proved to be a country walk accompanied by three dogs. Scott had been nervous of the animals at first, Teale told Briony.

'But there's not an ounce of vice in them. They've been very gentle with him. They seem to have taken to you too, especially Sally,' he said thoughtfully, looking down at the Springer spaniel plodding close at Briony's heels. Sally was the one who was heavy with pups.

'I'm sure animals know when someone likes them.' She paused to stroke the silky brown and white head and was rewarded with a liquid look of adoration. 'I've never actually owned a dog, but I'd like to some day. They're such good company.'

'Yes,' Teale agreed. 'I do most of my thinking, dreaming up plots and characters, when I'm walking these three.'

'I've often wondered...' Briony flushed at his quizzical glance. She hadn't meant to reveal just how frequently he was in her thoughts, but she went on, '...why you write horror fiction. Isn't there enough horror in the world?'

He tucked a companionable arm through hers and she fought to disguise the shudder of pleasure his touch induced.

'To a certain extent, I think reality *should* be mirrored in fiction. But you'll agree the kind I write is mostly escapist fantasy?'

'Yes,' she conceded a little breathlessly for, as they walked, their thighs brushed occasionally. 'And at least you always have good triumphing over evil.'

'I feel that's a moral obligation upon me as a widely read author. But I do like to disturb my readers a little, to make them look in a different way at things they've always taken for granted.'

'You may not like me saying this. But you and Matthew have more in common than you might think,' Briony told him. 'Yes,' she insisted, despite his wry grimace. 'Matthew's paintings disturb, make you look again, especially his red skies. When most people think of skies they automatically think of blue.'

They had reached woodland now. The Alsatian and the Dobermann surged ahead, scenting new pleasure. Briony would have expected a small boy to share their eagerness to explore.

'It's not natural,' she exclaimed. 'Look at him! He should be running wild, enjoying himself. He's just trotting along like a sedate little old man. When he came to the shop, it was days before I could get a word out of him.'

'From that, I gather he behaved himself? And,' with a twinkle, 'Promilla *didn't* object?'

'No, not a bit,' Briony returned his grin, 'once she was sure he wasn't going to get his fingers caught in the machines.'

She flushed a little as she recalled Promilla's comment when she'd heard about the weekend outing. 'Good move, Briony,' her friend had said. 'Get little Scott to look on you as a substitute for Charlene, and maybe his father will follow suit.'

'Does Scott talk to *you*?' she asked Teale.

'Very little,' he admitted.

A tumbling stream ran through the wooded valley, and Briony's artistic eye found a keen pleasure in the beauty of the autumn trees that flanked its chuckling course, not only in their shapes, seen to perfection now that the leaves were beginning to fall, but in their range of colours: deep pinks, greys, russet-browns and greens, one wood blending into another.

'Indescribably lovely,' Teale agreed when she enthused. He smiled self-deprecatingly. 'Perhaps *this* is why I write fantasy. It's impossible to do justice to the reality of nature. That's where you, as an artist, have the advantage.'

Earlier, the dogs had flushed out a clattering pheasant. Now Max, the Alsatian, disturbed a grey squirrel and set off in pursuit. The Dobermann followed, howling his excitement. At this, Scott showed his first reaction to his surroundings. His small face, his father's in miniature—how could Teale ever have doubted his parentage?—puckered woefully.

'Will they kill it?' he asked Briony.

'No, Scott.' She crouched on her haunches at the child's level. 'By now that little squirrel will be at the top of a tall tree.' She ventured to take the child's tense little fist in hers, and after a moment's hesitation she felt his fingers relax and curl confidingly about hers. He looked up at her, his grey eyes so like Teale's that Briony felt a spasm of love and longing for father and son run through her. But their acquaintance was not sufficiently advanced for her to give the child the embrace she longed to bestow. If only Scott were her son, hers and Teale's, she thought.

'It's a very long walk, isn't it?' he said with a heartfelt little sigh.

'Are you tired, darling?' When he nodded, she asked him, 'Shall we ask Daddy to carry you on his shoulder?' Unknowingly, the affection she felt sounded in her voice and, to the man watching, her manner with his son seemed admirably relaxed and easy-going, almost as though she were used to dealing with children.

With Scott now riding on Teale's shoulders, they emerged from the wood and followed the winding coastal track. The light was fading now, but it was not so dark that they could not see the tremendous seas. There was a cool little wind and lines of surf were forming far out, sweeping ashore in formidable waves.

'Winter's on its way,' said Teale, and then, as Briony gave an involuntary shiver, 'Hot muffins and some of Mrs Barrett's home-made cake in front of an enormous fire,' he promised.

As Teale had foretold, a log fire burnt cheerfully in the vast grate and within moments of their arrival, pleasantly tired from their afternoon in the fresh air, tea was brought in. To please Scott, they sat cross-legged on the thick pile rug, with only the firelight as illumination, while Teale toasted the muffins on the end of a long fork.

'No soulless oven grilling for me,' he told Briony. 'This is the proper way, the *only* way to toast muffins. Don't you agree?'

Right then, so long as Teale continued to look at her and smile like that, a contented Briony would have agreed that the moon was made from green cheese if it had pleased him to say so. She was unaware just how attractive she looked as she returned his smile, her red curls still windblown, her face warmed by the fire's radiance. Sally, the only one of the three dogs allowed into the drawing-room, lay stretched out as close to Briony as she could manage, giving little gusty sighs of pleasure as she alternately dozed and looked up at her newfound friend.

If only this moment could be fixed in time, Briony thought, stealing a surreptitious glance at Teale's austere profile etched against the firelight. If only every winter's afternoon could be spent like this in his company, but with her as his wife, with their children and animals around them.

'Penny for your thoughts?' he invited, catching her gaze upon him.

'Not worth it,' she lied.

'Or we don't know each other well enough yet for you to tell me, is that it?' he hazarded more accurately than he knew, and Briony held on to that little word 'yet' as a talisman for the future.

'My word! What a cosy family scene!' Rhoda arrived, bringing the cold evening air with her. Her dark good looks, so like her brother's, were enhanced by pinkened cheeks. She was glowing with health and energy, having walked from her cottage up to the big house. She was easily persuaded to join in what remained of their al-fresco meal. 'Am I taking Scott into the shop tomorrow, and have I got the car?' she asked her brother.

'If you don't mind, love? I've got a new idea I'm anxious to begin work on. In fact, you can take the car tonight if you like.'

'So that I don't have to interrupt the muse?' Rhoda enquired drily.

'Certainly not. I was thinking it would save you time in the morning.'

'In that case, it would save me even more time if Scott could spend the night at the cottage.' She turned to her nephew. 'Would you like that, lovey?'

'Yes, please, Auntie Rhoda. I like your little house. This house is very big.'

'Yes, love,' his aunt agreed, then *sotto voce* to her brother, echoing Briony's own thoughts, 'It needs filling with brothers and sisters.'

'No chance!' Teale said emphatically. 'One small boy is enough disruption in my working life.'

His sister threw him a withering look but made no further comment, probably because Scott was present.

'If we go now,' she suggested to the small boy, 'there'll be just time for a game with Libby before you go to bed.'

'Scott seems to have accepted Rhoda quite happily,' Briony said a little enviously as Teale's sister took the small boy to fetch his pyjamas and overnight things.

'I think her Libby's the attraction. At fifteen, she's still child enough to enjoy playing games with him.'

'Don't *you* play with him?'

Teale's eyebrows lifted comically. 'Don't you think I'm getting a little too long in the tooth for six-year-old games?'

'No!' Earnestly she shook her curly head at him. 'For one thing you're not that old, and for another I don't think you should ever be too old to play with your own children. I . . .'

'. . . speak from vast experience, of course!' he said teasingly, and Briony bit back what she had nearly said. She was relieved when Rhoda and Scott reappeared. The little boy was clutching a teddy bear nearly as large as himself. He looked small and vulnerable, and again Briony felt the urge to hug him.

'I ought to be going, too,' she said, albeit reluctantly.

'Surely there's no need for you to rush away?' Teale sounded surprised. 'Are you so busy? On a Sunday?'

'No.' And she wasn't in any hurry to leave. 'But you've got some writing you want to start.'

'Not until tomorrow. Today I set aside for Scott—and for you.' At his words, and aware of Rhoda's speculative gaze upon them, Briony's cheeks coloured becomingly. 'I'd planned for us to listen to some music, to see if our tastes coincide in that field, too,' he went on coaxingly.

'I'd take him up on it if I were you, Briony,' Rhoda advised. 'It's not often this brother of mine emerges from his monklike existence. You may not see him again for weeks on end. He's a real old grouch when he's in the middle of a book.'

'I can understand that,' Briony said. 'I hate leaving a painting when it's going well.'

With Rhoda's departure Briony was aware of a slight constraint. But perhaps it was merely on her side, for Teale seemed totally relaxed.

'Shall we make a pot of coffee before we settle down? Unless you'd like something stronger? Oh, but you don't drink,' he remembered.

'Not since my student days,' she told him. 'Coffee would be fine.'

'Anything to eat?'

'No.' That odd constriction was back in her throat. She knew she wouldn't be able to eat a morsel.

'Come and help me!' He held out his hand and, after a moment's hesitation, she took it and allowed him to lead her across the hall and through the baize door to the kitchen.

'I wait on myself at night,' he explained. 'Mrs Barrett's getting on. She goes to bed early. I suppose the day will come when I'll have to replace her. But I must admit

I'm not looking forward to it. She was here when my
parents were alive. She's a link with the past. Can you
understand that, or do you find it ridiculously
sentimental?'

She understood perfectly, and she told him so. It was
comforting, too, to find he had a core of sentimentality
beneath the independent façade he presented to the
world.

She watched as, surprisingly domesticated, quick and
deft in his movements, he moved around the well
equipped kitchen.

'You didn't really need my help,' she pointed out.

'No,' he admitted with a disarming grin. 'I just wanted
an admiring audience for my talents. Though I say it
myself, I do make a good cup of coffee.'

They returned to the drawing-room with their coffee;
it was excellent, and drinking it staved off the moment
when she must think of something to say. Teale mean-
while moved over to a powerful stereo. She watched him,
thinking that every time she saw him his looks were more
arresting than before, especially when a smile softened
his lean, chiselled features.

'What kind of music do you like?' he asked.

Briony had a varied taste but, brought suddenly from
her rapt contemplation of him, for the life of her she
couldn't think of a single composer or title.

'Oh—anything,' she floundered.

'Then I'll play you some of my favourites.' He put an
LP on the turntable, then came to sit beside her.

The music he had chosen was a Schumann symphony.
Briony knew it well. It was an inspirational piece she
often chose to listen to when painting. A charming,
lyrical work, it portrayed perfectly the joys and sorrows
of love and the feeling of the composer for natural
beauty. But this evening it filled her with nostalgia, with
the need for a closer sharing, to know strong arms around

her, but in particular to know the love of the man beside her. So strong was her need that she wondered he could not feel it emanating from her.

They sat in silence for a long while, until Teale broke it by saying, 'I had a long chat with Matthew yesterday.' It took Briony a moment to emerge from the mesmeric dream of sensuality that engulfed her. 'He's going down to London to see your contact about an exhibition.'

She forced herself to concentrate.

'Does he want anyone to go with him?'

'Strangely enough, no. I think Matthew may at last have found his feet. I hope so.'

'For his sake?' Briony enquired drily. 'Or for Rhoda's?'

'Both.' Teale took her hand, almost as if unaware that he did so, but his touch was enough to quicken her heartbeat. He gazed earnestly into her eyes. 'I agree with you, Briony. Matthew's had a raw deal out of life so far.' His thumb circled her palm as he spoke thoughtfully, and she was certain he had no idea of what the caress was doing to her already tautened senses. Her body clamoured to be nearer to him and it was all she could do to meet his eyes. 'I suppose I'm partly to blame. But I think we've come to an understanding. He genuinely loves my sister. I'm at last convinced of that.' He was silent for a moment, his eyes still consideringly on Briony's face, and an unbearable tension grew within her. How could he be so close and not sense that she was willing him to kiss her? She had literally to restrain herself from moving towards him and offering her lips, so certain was she the caress must eventually come. 'We all three have reason to be grateful to you, Briony.'

'I didn't really do anything,' she said breathlessly. Deep inside her sensation fluttered like a trapped bird. She felt dizzy, light-headed.

'You gave him an opportunity, encouraged him to find his true potential. On behalf of all of us, thank you, Briony.' With the hand he still held he pulled her nearer, then leant forward and put his lips to hers. His mouth was warm and gentle, the kiss almost tentative, but at its touch sensation exploded within her.

With a little sob of gladness she moved closer to him, her free hand curling about the nape of his neck. She seemed to have been waiting a lifetime for this kiss. Her lips parted, inviting his invasion, and she heard his quick intake of breath. His kiss deepened and she was conscious of his tensing muscles and of the shudder that went through him. But then, unbelievably, he captured the hand that had entwined itself in his hair and put her gently away from him.

'I'm sorry. That wasn't meant to happen.' He said it as though it had been his fault, but she knew it hadn't been and the heat of shame swept through her.

'No,' she forced a laugh, 'it wasn't.' She gathered the remnants of her pride. 'I'm sorry, too. Put it down to Schumann!' She aimed for flippancy. 'I always was a sucker for mood music.'

She thought his responding laugh held relief. Her mouth had gone dry and there was a sickness in her stomach. She felt close to tears. She had to get away before she made a complete fool of herself. It took all her self-control to make her movements leisurely as she stretched, yawned and looked at her wristwatch, feigning surprise.

'Goodness! And it's Monday tomorrow! I'd better not be any later.'

It seemed to her that he followed her lead with unflattering alacrity, his manner formal.

'Thank you for giving up so much of your day. I do appreciate it.' He escorted her to the door and as punctiliously saw her to her car.

'Goodnight.' With the engine running, she waited fractionally, giving him the chance to suggest they meet again, but nothing was forthcoming, and a depression that was beyond tears settled over her as she accelerated away.

CHAPTER SIX

'Oh, Prom! I made a damned fool of myself tonight.'

'Nonsense! From what you've told me, I think you carried it off very well.'

'It's taught me a lesson. From now on, I'm going to forget Teale Munro. I'm going to steer clear of him and his family.'

'That's not going to be easy,' Promilla pointed out, 'with Matthew and Rhoda working upstairs, little Scott coming in with them. And what about the painting of his house? If I know you, you won't leave that unfinished.'

'Well, all right!' Even with her friend, Briony couldn't keep the exasperation from her voice. 'I'll steer clear of *him*, then. And *that* shouldn't be difficult. After tonight, *he'll* be avoiding *me* like the plague!'

Briony might declare she was going to forget Teale, but it was impossible, not only in her own heart, but since she couldn't avoid hearing the mention of his name.

'Did you enjoy the rest of the evening?' was the first thing Rhoda asked her next morning. Since it was Monday, Briony had decided to do some painting herself. On the canvas before her, the outlines of the gracious old house were slowly taking shape. She would be glad to finish it and be rid of it, she told herself. Matthew had gone for his usual check-up, so Briony and Rhoda had the studio to themselves.

'Oh—yes—er—it was all right. Actually, I didn't stay long after you left.' She sensed Rhoda's surprise.

However, the other woman went on, 'It's good to see Teale taking an interest in someone at long last. After the business with Charlene I was afraid he'd never...'

'Oh, but there's nothing like that,' Briony said quickly. 'In fact, I doubt if I'll be seeing him again.' She bent over her work, but she was aware of Rhoda's grey eyes fixed intently on her averted profile.

'Is that *your* decision?' the other woman asked finally. 'Forgive me if I seem to be prying, but I'm very fond of my brother. He's looked happier these past weeks than I've seen him in a long time. I wouldn't like him to be hurt again.'

'He won't be hurt by me,' Briony assured her. It pained her to admit it, but she forced herself to say, 'It was only this business of Matthew that threw us together. Now that's sorted out...' She shrugged, because she couldn't trust her voice not to quiver if she went on.

Rhoda said no more and Briony made an effort to seem her usual cheerful self, but throughout the day she was aware of the other woman's speculative glances.

In the weeks that followed, Promilla too seemed to be continually concerned for Briony's welfare. Finally, her solicitous enquiries drove Briony to an uncharacteristically sharp retort.

'For God's sake, Prom! I'm not going into a decline just because I mistook a man's friendliness for something more. Forget the whole thing. I have,' she said mendaciously.

Obligingly, Promilla changed the subject. 'Have you heard from Iseult yet about Christmas?'

'No.' That was another cause for discontent. 'I hope Jean-Luc will let her come. If I don't hear soon, I shall telephone his Paris office.'

Only one thing occurred to lighten Briony's mood. One Tuesday morning, early in November, she was alone in the shop. Promilla was out on a delivery; Rhoda had

not come in. She had telephoned apologetically from
the nearest call-box to the cottage to say that little Scott
was suffering from a heavy cold and that she didn't feel
it would be wise to bring him out into the cold November
weather. Why couldn't Teale look after his own sick
child? Briony fumed. That was just typical of him—total
non-involvement, even with his own son. In her heart,
she knew he was probably engrossed with his latest book;
and from personal experience she could understand his
distancing himself from everyone and everything. But
she'd found the only way to deal with her pain was to
goad herself to anger with him, to persuade herself he
was totally unlikeable, that she was better off without
him. The doorbell jangled and she looked up from the
soft toys she was pricing. There would soon be a demand
for them with Christmas coming up.

'Good morning. Can I help you?' She looked expectantly at the tall man in jeans and sweater who had entered, leaving the door open behind him. He was
hovering in front of the counter. He wasn't remarkably
good-looking, but he had a pleasant, clean-shaven face
and a nicely shaped head, the brown hair cut closely to
its line. His tall, rangy frame was erect and self-confident.

'You already have, more than you'll ever know.'

Briony frowned. Was he a line-shooter? She was in
no mood for flirtatious repartee.

'Briony?' He sounded vastly amused. 'Don't you re-
cognise me?'

Something in his voice made her look at him more
closely, then she gave a little squeal of surprise. She
rounded the counter and dragged him over to the better
light near the window.

'Matthew! You've shaved off your beard!'

'And had a haircut. Do you think it's an improvement?' he asked with a trace of his old diffidence.

'I didn't mind the beard,' she told him frankly. 'But yes, I think I like the new you. It suits your up-and-coming image.'

'An image I'd never have had but for you. I'm an artist, a *real* honest-to-goodness artist at last,' he said exultantly. 'I'm going to have an exhibition. And yesterday they finally signed me off at the hospital.' He seemed to have forgotten Briony wasn't supposed to know about his illness.

'Oh, Matthew!' she said softly. 'I'm so glad for you.'

'This is from me—and Rhoda.' Unexpectedly, he grabbed her in a bear hug and lifted her from the floor. He swung her round in a crazy dance of celebration and concluded it with a resounding kiss full on her lips.

As he set her down and she laughed up at him, she saw his eyes fixed on something behind her. His expression was one of irritated resignation. She turned to see what had caught his attention and found herself looking straight into Teale's face as he stood in the open doorway. She couldn't think of anything to say, but almost instinctively she backed towards Matthew, as if seeking protection, and saw Teale's lip curl.

But Teale did not level the expected accusation at them. Instead, he jerked his head towards the stairs. 'Is Rhoda up there?'

Briony found her voice. 'She's not in today. But you must know that? Scott's sick.'

'No, I didn't know. No one saw fit to tell *me*.'

'Perhaps she was afraid of "disturbing" your work,' Briony couldn't keep the sarcasm from her voice. Inwardly, she was shaking. At the sight of him, all her feelings for him had surged over her so that she was afraid of betraying herself. She *had* to hide behind antagonism.

Teale seemed untouched by her sarcasm. He directed his question to Matthew. 'How sick *is* the boy?'

'Nothing drastic. Just a cold. But Rhoda worries about him.'

Teale nodded. But he seemed relieved, Briony thought. She supposed he must be fond of Scott in his own rather distant way.

'At least seeing you will save me a trip. But I wish to goodness you'd agree to have the telephone put in at the cottage. Tell Rhoda I have to go up to London. I don't know how long I'll be away. If she wants me, a message left at the flat will find me eventually.'

'Oh, but . . .' Matthew began, but Teale was already on his way out of the door.

'Can't stop. I've got a train to catch.' He nodded a brusque farewell that encompassed both of them.

'Damn! Damn! Damn!' Matthew exploded.

'It's all right, Matthew,' Briony reassured him, though she wasn't altogether certain herself. 'I'm sure he didn't think . . .'

'I'm not worried about what he *thought*,' Matthew interrupted. 'I'm annoyed at what he's *done*. I wanted to go up to London myself the day after tomorrow and take Rhoda with me. The chappie at the gallery wants to meet her and take us both out for a slap-up meal. I planned to make a long weekend of it. The first chance I get to do something really good for Rhoda, and now she's going to be stuck at home with Teale's boy!'

'Perhaps Teale will be back in time.'

'I doubt it,' Matthew said gloomily. 'You heard him. It's not as if he's got any reason to rush home, either.' Briony winced. 'Oh, well, I'd better get back to the cottage and tell Rhoda the trip's off.'

'She knows about it?'

'Yes.' Gloomily, he added, 'She's already planning what she's going to wear.'

'Look, Matthew,' Briony said hesitantly as he moved towards the door. 'Perhaps I could help. Promilla and

I could help,' she amended. 'If Teale isn't back in time, you could leave Scott here. He's used to both of us now and it's not as if he's any trouble.'

'It seems a bit of an imposition,' Matthew said doubtfully, but his face had brightened.

'Not a bit.' Briony was firm. There would be a poignant pain in looking after Teale's son, but it would be a shame for Rhoda and Matthew to be cheated of their first real treat in years.

Though Scott was at school by day, he settled happily into staying at the Blue Unicorn. He was obviously fascinated by the varied and exotic furnishings that decked the girls' living quarters, and was soon fast friends with Briony's cats. Briony had made up a bed for him on a put-you-up in a corner of her own room.

There was an exquisite pleasure in undressing and bathing a small child again, in leaning over the tiny sleeping form to gently kiss his brow before she retired herself. On the second morning of his stay, Scott surprised her by creeping into her bed and snuggling up to her.

'Hello, darling!' she greeted him. 'This is nice!'

'I wish I lived with you and Auntie Promilla all the time.'

'You've got Auntie Rhoda,' she reminded him.

'Mmmn,' he agreed. 'But Auntie Rhoda has Libby and Uncle Matthew. You and Auntie Promilla haven't got any children or daddies to keep you company. Wouldn't you like me to live with you always, Auntie Briony?'

'Oh yes, darling,' she breathed, 'I'd like that very much.'

'Of course, there wouldn't be room here for Daddy.' Scott looked around consideringly. A sudden idea struck him and he sat bolt upright. 'But you could come and live with me and my daddy. There's plenty of room at Daddy's house.'

A pang smote Briony, and she held the small boy close for a moment, her eyes tightly closed against the sting of sudden tears. If only it were that simple!

'But then poor Promilla would be all on her own,' she pointed out, careful to keep her voice light.

'She could come, too.' Scott was prodigal with his father's house.

It was a good thing children's minds were easily diverted, Briony mused when she'd successfully suggested it was time they got up and gave the cats their breakfast.

'We're in charge of the shop today,' she reminded the child.

Promilla had asked if Briony minded her being away over the weekend.

'I'd thought of going up to London. I want to look up the Patis, old friends of my parents.'

'Of course you must go,' Briony had told her. 'It's about time you had a day or two off.'

It was not particularly busy for a Saturday. The tourist season was long over, and people had not yet launched themselves into a frenzy of Christmas shopping. There was ample time to entertain a small boy. And to grow to love him more by the minute, which wasn't very wise, Briony told herself. But how could she help it? It wasn't just that Scott was Teale's son; he was an appealing child and Briony had a strong maternal nature which had been too long suppressed.

The shop closed earlier on Saturdays, and after tea Briony had a sudden impulse to sketch Scott as he played with the cats. Her skilful pencil filled sheet after sheet with swift impressions; and, when for a short while he fell asleep, she was able to make a more detailed drawing of his head.

She made the most of the bedtime ritual. Scott's bath was followed by a story during which, inevitably, the small boy fell asleep. She tucked him in, lingering lovingly over the task, smoothing back the dark curls from the soft skin of his forehead. It was going to be torture to give him up when Rhoda returned tomorrow evening; and she sat up late, dreaming over the fire, reluctant to go to bed and thus bring tomorrow nearer.

She must have fallen asleep, for she woke with a start. The fire had burned down and the room was chilly. Confused, she sat for a moment, wondering what had disturbed her. Had Scott cried out in his sleep? She tiptoed into the bedroom, but all was peaceful. Then she heard the prolonged peal of the doorbell, as though someone had their finger pressed hard and continuously upon it. Someone was pounding on the wooden panels of the shop door.

Briony was alarmed. She was alone except for a small child, and while Gwinvercombe was relatively free of crime, one could never be certain. Stealthily, without revealing a light, she crept through into the shop and peered through a corner of the window blind. In the darkened street all she could be sure of was the outline of a man. Then a passing car caught him for an instant in its headlights, and she recognised Teale. What was he doing here at this time? It was after midnight. With trembling fingers, she unbolted the door. Unbidden visions crossed her mind. Perhaps there had been some miraculous transformation in him, and he'd been possessed by an irresistible urge to see her.

'Teale?' Her voice was husky.

'Briony! Thank God! What's going on? Where *is* everyone? Where's Scott?'

'He's here, but ...'

'Here? What in God's name is he doing here?' He marched past her and into the rear of the shop.

Briony fastened the door and hurried after him.

'He's in bed, asleep. Don't waken him.'

In the electric light, Teale's face was drawn and tired. New lines seemed etched at the corners of his eyes and mouth.

'I got the last train down from London, took a taxi out to my place to find it all closed up. No Mrs Barrett. No dogs. No food. No explanation.' He dropped down on to the sofa in an attitude of exhaustion and ran a hand around the back of his neck, massaging tense muscles. 'Then I went down to the cottage, only to find that empty, too. It was beginning to feel like the *Mary Celeste*. To top it all, I found the Rolls had developed a flat. I had to change a wheel before I could drive over here.'

'I'm sorry you were worried, but no one was expecting you back so soon,' Briony told him from the kitchen doorway. Seeing his fatigue, she had switched on the coffee percolator. 'Mrs Barrett's gone to see her niece in Paignton. The dogs are boarded out at one of the farms. Matthew and Rhoda are in London.' She explained the circumstances of their trip and her offer to look after Scott. 'Have you eaten lately?' she asked Teale as she handed him a mug of coffee.

'Not since I left London. But I'm not hungry, just damnably tired.' He sat hunched forward, his hands clasped about the mug as though he were cold as well as weary, and Briony sensed depression in his mood.

She knelt in front of the fire, stirred its glowing embers into new life and threw on a couple of logs.

'London *can* be tiring.' She sat back on her heels and studied his drawn face.

'I've been to see Charlene,' he said abruptly.

'Oh!' She averted her face and made a great play of poking the fire. How, she asked herself fiercely, could

she be so despicable as to be jealous of a dying woman?
'How is she?'

'Very poorly. I've been sitting up with her at night,
to give her mother a break.' He went on, speaking
rapidly, the words pouring out of him as if he needed
to unburden himself. 'It's the least I could do, isn't it?
God knows, our marriage was a mistake. But its failure
wasn't entirely her fault.' He ran an impatient hand
through his hair, dishevelling its dark thickness. 'I should
never have married, of course. Not just Charlene, but
anyone.' He looked at Briony, her face still in profile to
him, long lashes sweeping her cheeks. 'Do you know
what George Bernard Shaw said about writers?' And
bitterly, as Briony shook her head and turned to look
wonderingly at him, he continued, 'He said they'd let
their wives starve, their children go barefoot, their
mothers drudge for their living, so long as *they* were free
to write. That's the sort of man I seem to have become.'
He sounded genuinely horrified. 'Oh, my family didn't
lack for material comforts, but they were starved of my
attention. I know this, and yet I can't stop writing any
more than I could voluntarily stop breathing.'

'I think you're being too hard on yourself, Teale,'
Briony told him gently, knowing the need to comfort the
tortured man before her. 'Marriage shouldn't be a prison.
People are still entitled to their own identity.'

His smile was weary. 'Yes. Being an artist, *you* would
understand that. I think that's why I find it so easy to
talk to you. We're two of a kind, you and I. You value
your freedom, too.' Briony flinched; if only he knew!
'But have *you* ever been married?'

Briony flinched again. At her side, her small hands
balled into tight fists.

'No.'

'Then you can't know what it's like. It isn't that easy. Partners feel entitled to make demands on your time. They don't understand the compulsion to...'

'But surely——' out of her own values and beliefs, Briony felt bound to protest '—people don't get married in the first place unless they enjoy each other's company?'

'You think not?' His expression was cynical. 'Sometimes I ask myself just why I got married. If I'm honest, wasn't I just attracted to a pretty face and a sexy body? Wasn't marriage just the price I had to pay for possessing both? Certainly, it seems there was nothing else.'

'In that case,' Briony said firmly, 'if you'll forgive me for saying so, you married the wrong person. There *has* to be more than just physical attraction. There has to be liking, respect, mutual interests.'

'Is that why *you've* never married?' he asked curiously. 'Because you've never met anyone that embodied all those things?' As she nodded, he went on thoughtfully, 'You may be right, of course. But I don't believe the woman exists who could offer me all that.' Wryly, he added, 'But at least I never make the same mistake twice.' He yawned and leant back on the sofa, his long body suddenly more relaxed. 'You're a good listener, Briony. It's good to be able to talk to someone who understands, who *doesn't* make demands. Do you know, I believe I *am* hungry,' he told her. 'You wouldn't have the odd sandwich or slice of cake going begging?' His tone of voice and his lop-sided smile had all the coaxing appeal of his son's when asking a favour, and Briony's heart lurched. If only he weren't so damnably attractive. If only *she* could think of *him* just as a friend, as he treated her.

'I'll make you something.'

But when she returned from the kitchen Teale was asleep. Softly she put down the tray she carried. For a long moment she stood looking at him, hungrily studying the familiar features. Then she tiptoed into the bedroom and returned with a thick blanket. Careful not to disturb him, she eased his long legs up on to the sofa and spread the blanket over him. She longed to smooth back the dark hair from his brow, as she had done earlier for his son, but she didn't want to wake him. If she did, he might go, and for just these few hours she wanted him here under the same roof as herself. She wanted to pretend he belonged here, that he belonged to her, even though there was no future in such imaginings.

'Good morning! Room service, madam!'

'Wh-what?' Sleepily, Briony raised herself on one elbow, red curls in disarray, the thin straps of her night-dress slipping from her shoulder, revealing the gentle curves and swell of her breasts. Her skin was of a creamy paleness often found in redheads. In an appealingly childish gesture, she knuckled sleep from her eyes and then stared disbelievingly.

Teale stood in the open doorway to her bedroom. He held a tray and there was the tantalisingly fragrant smell of fresh coffee and toast.

'I don't know if you're a breakfast eater,' he said cheerily, 'but I'm starving.'

Briony continued to stare at him. Obviously he had showered, for his dark hair was still damp. Curls slicked wetly about his brow and neck. He was wearing a towel-ling robe that belonged to Promilla. It was just about the right width. But the length! Three-quarters on her plump friend, it reached barely to mid-thigh on Teale.

He followed the direction of her gaze, down over muscular, hair-roughened legs, and his smile became rueful.

'It was all I could find.' He moved towards the bed.

Mesmerised, Briony watched as he set the tray on the bedside table. There were two cups, two plates and he had toasted what must be nearly half a loaf of bread. He sat on the edge of the bed, close enough for her to touch if she'd had the courage. Belatedly, she remembered her scanty attire and pulled the sheet up around her shoulders, catching his amused smile. Swallowing, she dragged her eyes away from him and looked towards the corner put-you-up, where his son had slept.

'Where's Scott?'

Teale jerked his head in the direction of the kitchen.

'Out there, demolishing a couple of boiled eggs. His appetite has certainly improved.' As he spoke, Teale poured coffee.

Briony took her cup with a tremulous hand. She was wide awake now, but she still felt unprepared to cope with the unexpectedness of his presence in her room, here actually sitting on the side of her bed. If only the apparent intimacy of this breakfast *à deux* were the real thing, she thought wistfully. If only Teale had just left her bed, and would soon be returning to it to make love to her once more before a new day began. She felt her cheeks go pink, and it was an effort to meet his eyes when he spoke again.

'Thanks for the overnight refuge and for listening to my morbid ramblings. You're a good pal, Briony! I don't think I *could* have driven home last night. I was absolutely whacked.' As he munched toast and sipped coffee he looked about him with interest, and Briony found herself seeing her room as if for the first time, through his eyes.

If the living quarters were an amalgam of the two girls' interests, Briony's bedroom was uniquely her own. Soft Laura Ashley prints gave it a golden aura that in the subdued lighting gave emphasis to the creaminess of her skin, the vital copper of her hair. There was a wealth of colour, texture and pattern. One wall held a collection of exquisitely executed water-colours, the work of an aged great-aunt from whom Briony supposed she must have inherited her love of art.

'A brass bed?' Teale said questioningly, his gaze returning to Briony.

'Not the genuine article, I'm afraid. It's only reproduction. I'd never be able to afford the real thing. But the quilt——' she stroked it lovingly '—is real. One of Prom's auction-room finds.'

'Ah yes, that reminds me. Auctions. There's a supposedly good one towards the end of next week, down Bideford way. Would you like to go? It would mean an early start. We might even combine it with some more sight-seeing.'

'Sight-seeing?' she laughed. 'In November?'

But Briony felt as though she'd been offered the Crown Jewels. She was careful, though, to moderate her pleasure. If Teale suspected for one moment that she felt anything more for him than friendship, he would withdraw again behind his barriers. To him, she thought wistfully, she was just 'a good pal'.

'But you'll come?' As she nodded, unaware of the revealing light in her eyes, he muttered, 'Briony...' He leant towards her, his tone suddenly urgent, and Briony's heart pounded in her breast, her quickened breathing disturbing the lacy edging of her nightdress. 'I...'

'Briony,' a small voice said plaintively, and Scott appeared in the doorway, a large slice of toast clutched in his hand, 'when are you getting up? Tara and Stripey want their breakfast, and I can't open the tin.'

'I think,' Briony's voice was a little shaky, 'we'll ask Daddy to open the tin while I get up.'

She hadn't imagined that moment of tension, she told herself as she showered and dressed. If only Scott's ar-

rival had been delayed by a second or two more, she
might have known what Teale had been going to say.

With a happy small boy seated between them, delighted to be in the company of his two favourite people,
and the satisfied cats purring on the hearth, breakfast
was a pleasant meal. It was almost possible to imagine
they were a family, Briony thought as she looked from
Teale's face to that of his son.

The occasion must have reminded Scott of yesterday's
conversation for suddenly he said, 'Daddy, I wish Briony
lived with us always. She could be my new mummy,
couldn't she?' Then, as Briony wondered whether her
heart really had stopped beating, he looked at her appealingly. 'Auntie Rhoda said my real mummy's soon
going up to heaven to live with the angels, so *she* won't
be able to live with me.'

Briony dared not look at Teale. The blood seemed to
be pounding in her face and head, deafening her so that
his words seemed to come from a long way off. But his
tone was even and matter-of-fact as he said, 'Briony's
a very busy lady. She hasn't got time to be anyone's
mummy. I'm afraid you'll have to settle for her being
an auntie.'

Briony found her voice. 'Will that do, Scott?' she
asked still avoiding Teale's gaze.

'Is an auntie as special as a mummy?' he said
doubtfully.

'Almost.' She nearly choked on the single word, and
indulged in a fit of coughing to disguise its cause. 'Cereal
went the wrong way,' she croaked when Scott obligingly
patted her on the back.

'Would an auntie live with us?' Scott asked his father.
'Because when I was in London with Mummy I had a
lot of uncles and they stayed with us, in Mummy's room.
Mummy said it was because we hadn't enough bedrooms. But *we've* got a lot of bedrooms, haven't we,

Daddy? So Auntie Briony wouldn't have to share yours. Unless, of course,' he added generously, 'she wanted to.'

'Time I was on my way,' Teale announced, pushing back his chair. 'You said Rhoda's due back tonight? Is it OK if Scott stays till then?' He seemed in a sudden hurry to depart.

That's right, Briony thought indignantly, leave me to answer the awkward questions! Aloud, she said, 'Of course he can stay.'

She accompanied him to the door. She'd been hoping he'd stay a little longer, she thought forlornly. In fact, she'd hoped he'd remain all day. She'd looked forward to making his meals, perhaps watching television together or taking a walk. But perhaps that smacked too much of the domesticity Teale deplored. Undoubtedly Scott's ingenuous remarks had embarrassed him.

'I'll be in touch—about the auction,' he said as he took his leave, and her heart lifted just a little.

'Keep your eyes open for antique lace and linens. Some of these old farmers' wives are notorious hoarders,' Promilla adjured Briony as she waited for Teale to arrive a few days later. The auction near Bideford was to consist of effects from two or three farmhouses from surrounding areas. 'And,' she added with a wicked twinkle in her eyes, 'don't let the love-light blind you to any defects.'

Small chance of that, Briony thought as the Rolls pulled away up the steep hill out of Gwinvercombe. Teale's greeting had been polite, even friendly, but by no stretch of the imagination could it have been called loverlike.

'Did Promilla enjoy her weekend in London?' he enquired after a particularly long silence which Briony found herself powerless to break.

'Very much,' she said, relieved by the introduction of this non-controversial subject. 'She's been thinking lately of visiting an elderly great-aunt in Karachi. Now we've got Rhoda to help out with the sewing, she's finally made up her mind to go—over Christmas and the New Year.'

'Alone?'

'No. I think that's what finally decided her. She visited some old friends of her parents and they told her their son was off to Karachi shortly to see his grandparents. They offered his services as an escort.'

'So you'll be alone over Christmas?'

She waited breathlessly for him to extend an invitation, but none was forthcoming.

'Not quite alone. At least, I hope not. I've invited . . . someone to spend a few days with me. I haven't heard yet whether or not they can come.'

Then he raised the subject she'd been dreading. 'I'm sorry,' he said brusquely, 'if Scott's remarks the other day embarrassed you.'

'Oh!' she said swiftly, then added untruthfully, 'I wasn't embarrassed, just amused. Children see things in such an uncomplicated way.'

'Yes.' He sounded relieved. 'What sort of stuff will you be looking for today?' he asked, and the conversation moved into safer channels.

The auction room, an enormous apartment behind an estate agent's office, was crammed with articles for sale and with prospective purchasers. There was an hour before the sale was due to start, to give buyers a chance to examine the various lots. Briony and Teale had already decided that they would split up for this exercise, meeting again at a pre-arranged point to confer before the bidding began. It was a pity they hadn't been able to come for the viewing on the previous day, Briony thought as she struggled through the press of people and tried to examine lot numbers without giving away her interest. She made surreptitious notes on her catalogue of the prices she was prepared to pay.

'Looks as if we'll be here all day,' Teale commented as they compared notes. Happily, Briony reflected that she wouldn't mind if the proceedings took a week, so long as she could be with Teale. The press and jostle of people around them meant that they were forced to stand close together, and several times Teale had to steady her as someone struggled for a better vantage point. 'Fortunately, the auctioneer breaks at one o'clock for lunch,' Teale went on. 'If possible, we'll slip out before that, because there'll be an absolute stampede for the only pub.'

The bidding started slowly with the miscellanea which Briony always found tedious. Outdoor items, garden tools, old cookers and electric fires. But at last the action moved to the quality pieces and from then on it was fast and furious. Teale had several pieces of antique furniture knocked down to him, including another harmonium which Briony would dearly have loved to possess. But even if Teale hadn't been bidding for it himself the price soared far beyond her range. She was successful, however, in obtaining the materials Promilla wanted.

'Anything else you want to bid on before lunch?' Teale asked; as she shook her head, he suggested, 'Right, let's get over there before the rush.'

The Sir Walter Raleigh was already busy, but they managed to find a corner seat. Briony looked around her appreciatively. She loved the atmosphere of old hostelries: the dark oak beams, the glint of brass and copper. She had always enjoyed watching people, too, and this she did, wishing she'd thought to bring a sketchbook, while Teale fought his way to the bar to order their meal.

This consisted of a very creditable steak, though Briony groaned over the inevitable chips.

'I shouldn't have thought you had to worry about your figure,' Teale said. It was the nearest he'd ever come to a personal remark. If, Briony thought, you discounted those he'd made at their first encounter, when she'd found his open appraisal of her femininity decidedly insulting.

But over lunch his conversation consisted of generalities about topical themes, such as the auction, and Briony asked him about the book he was currently writing. Since she'd met Teale, she'd re-read those of his books she possessed with greater attention, looking for the man she knew behind the author. She thought perhaps Teale's own attitudes were revealed in the cynicism of his characters, particularly with regard to male/female relationships.

'Is it going well?'

'No, dammit! And I can't think why. I know what I want to write about, the characters are clear in my mind. I'm working under the usual conditions. Rhoda's being a brick and keeping Scott out of my hair. And yet I find myself unable to concentrate. Normally I wouldn't break off for a day out like this, but I found the more I tried to overcome the block the worse it got.'

'Maybe, subconsciously, you're worrying about something?' Briony suggested.

'Hmmph,' he grunted. 'Maybe. But if I am it must be buried pretty deep down. I've had something on my mind, I grant you. But I wouldn't say it had been worrying me exactly.' But he did not offer to confide in her.

The afternoon bidding saw several more lots attributed to Teale, and Briony was successful in obtaining some items of antique jewellery. But by mid-afternoon they felt they had done sufficiently well. Payment made and delivery of their purchases arranged, Teale suggested they make for home, stopping off somewhere for afternoon tea. He was very quiet on the return journey and Briony respected his uncommunicative mood. She wondered if he was thinking about his book or whether he was mulling over the undeclared subject which he had denied was a problem.

He made only one remark before they stopped for tea, shooting her an oblique glance as he did so. 'You're a very restful person to be with, Briony. A lot of women seem to find it necessary to gabble on continuously.'

'I've always thought there's such a thing as a companionable silence,' Briony said serenely.

'Exactly. But it's rare to find someone capable of observing it.'

A slight detour took them to Appledore, one of Teale's favourite villages, he revealed, and he suggested they look around before the light failed. With its narrow streets and lanes, it was a place to be explored on foot and it had a history to be discovered. The churchyard was filled with the graves of those who had given their lives to the sea—captains, pilots and master mariners. Old cottages were decorated with figureheads or inscribed plates above their doorways. Later, they found a small café which served Devonshire cream teas, and Briony was surprised and dismayed to discover how fast time was moving.

'Do you never wish,' she asked Teale in an unguarded moment, 'that you could stop the clock at a point where you're really enjoying yourself?'

He considered her question.

'I suppose I must have done, in the past. But I can't say there have been many such moments of late.'

And that puts you firmly in your place, she told herself wryly.

CHAPTER SEVEN

TEALE redeemed himself, however, as they made their way back to the car. He stopped suddenly and looked down at Briony.

'What a boor you must think me!' As she looked at him enquiringly, he explained, 'I've just realised, back there you paid me a compliment. At least, I assume you meant you were enjoying today? My company?' Briony nodded somewhat ruefully. 'I'm sorry, Briony, I really am. Please don't think *I* haven't enjoyed today, because I have, immensely. I suppose when I answered your question I was thinking more of earth-shattering moments which, let's face it, don't occur that frequently.' He stopped and grinned lop-sidedly at her. 'Am I making things worse?'

'Of course not,' she assured him. 'I know exactly what you mean.'

'Look,' he said as he held the car door open for her, 'don't let's end the day with me dropping you off in Gwinvercombe. Come back to the house. Scott will be thrilled to see you, and later we'll listen to more music and I'll rustle us up some supper. How does that strike you?'

If she'd had any pride, Briony supposed she'd have made some plausible excuse. She'd already given him pretty good reason to suppose she didn't want this day in his company to end. But where Teale was concerned she didn't seem to *have* much pride.

'I'd like that,' she said instead.

In the event, she saw very little of Scott, for it was nearly his bedtime when they reached the manor house. But she was able to tuck him into his bed and promise she would see him again very soon.

'Poor little mite,' she said to Teale when she came downstairs. 'Do you think he misses his mother too dreadfully?'

'At times, I imagine.' Teale ushered her into the drawing-room and moved to put a record on the stereo. 'How about some Mozart tonight?' As she nodded, he sat beside her and reverted to the subject of his son. 'But he seems a well enough adjusted child, and he has Rhoda as a substitute. Oh,' as Briony drew in a slightly disapproving breath at his casual manner, 'I do my best, naturally. I'm not a monster. I'm fond of the boy, but I *am* a busy man. Which is why...' He was on his feet again, restlessly circuiting the room. 'Look, Briony, about what Scott said the other day... He dropped a bit of a clanger, didn't he?'

She didn't pretend to misunderstand. 'I told you, it didn't bother me. He's only a little boy. He can't be expected to understand...'

'True,' he nodded, 'but we're *not* children. And I think the time has come for plain speaking between us.' He said it without looking at her.

Waiting in the tense atmosphere that filled the room for him to continue, Briony felt she could hardly breathe.

'Over the last couple of months I've come to value your friendship, Briony. You're talented, intelligent, good company—and something more. You also have integrity.' He hadn't complimented her on her looks, Briony thought wryly. 'So much so,' he went on, 'that I feel I can be entirely honest with you.'

'You always have been. You've told me a lot about yourself; things you needn't have told me.' She was suddenly afraid of what he might be about to say.

'Things that very few people know about. But that's you, Briony.' He paused for a moment and studied her face, his own expression inscrutable, then went on, 'You seem to draw me out. It's years since I talked to anyone the way I've talked to you these past weeks.' He was silent for so long that Briony began to feel uncomfortable under the scrutiny of intent grey eyes, began to wonder if he'd changed his mind about revealing himself further. But then he came back to sit beside her and, to her amazement and disconcertion, he took one of her hands in both of his.

He did not meet her eyes, but instead looked down at the hand he held, his thumb absently caressing its palm. The music soared to an exquisite crescendo of sound. Sensuality, sharp and sweet, stabbed through her as she stared at his dark, downbent head. There was a stillness between them that seemed to be waiting only for the right word or gesture to break it. All her senses urged her to reach out and touch him. But something held her back from doing so.

'Briony,' his voice throbbed strangely and at his next words she tingled the length of her spine, 'I can't deny that I also find you very attractive—physically. There have been moments when I've believed you felt the same way?'

She wanted to respond to him, but some instinct of self-preservation kept her silent.

'No, dammit!' His head jerked up and he stared into widened blue eyes. 'If I'm being honest, let me be *totally* honest.' There was a moment of charged intensity, then Teale said forcefully, 'I want you, Briony. The moment I clapped eyes on you that first day in the shop I felt it. It was there, all mixed up with the anger, the contempt. It made me even angrier that I should be attracted to you—to Matthew's mistress, as I thought you were then. Then, when I found out you weren't ... Since then, I've fought against it. I even stopped seeing you at one point, because I didn't want to get involved. But when I wasn't with you I found myself thinking about you. I told you today something was coming between me and my writing. I pretended I didn't know what it was. But I can't pretend any more, not even to myself. It's you, Briony. I stare at a blank sheet of paper and find myself seeing you. I try to write lines of dialogue and instead I find myself talking to you, telling you...wondering if...Briony, if I'm not to remain in that state for ever what I need to know is, do *you* want *me*?'

'Teale,' she began, 'I...'

'No, let me finish. I think I've told you enough about myself for you to realise I'm essentially a loner? Experience has proved that. There's no way I can commit myself to any permanent relationship.'

'Yes, I know.' Briony's voice was muffled. She felt suddenly choked by tears, for she knew what was coming.

'As I said, I've thought sometimes that you weren't altogether indifferent to me? *Do* you care enough for me to accept the little I *can* offer? Or was I mistaken? Don't you care for me at all?' He looked searchingly at her flushed face and unconsciously quivering lips, and it was Briony's turn to lower her eyes.

Her thoughts raced desperately. She loved him, more than she'd ever loved anyone else in the whole of her life. She wanted him, too. But there was more to it than that: she needed him far more than he could possibly need her, for she also needed the sustaining warmth of *permanent* love.

'Briony?'

She thought he was pressing her for her answer, and she looked up at the precise moment that he reached for her and pulled her almost roughly into his arms.

'Perhaps you need help making up your mind,' he murmured huskily. 'Let me show you how it is with *me*.'

His kiss was sensuous, searching, reinforcing his claim that he needed her.

If it occurred to Briony to resist, the instinct lasted only a brief second. She had waited so long for this moment and her mouth was sweet and softly parted beneath his.

His fingers plunged into the thickness of her red curls, moved sensuously in, around and behind her ears. As the kiss continued, he captured one of her hands and pressed it against his chest, then undid the buttons of his shirt.

'Touch me, Briony,' he muttered. 'For God's sake, touch me.'

His skin was hair-roughened, warm and slightly moist, and as she explored the muscled contours she could feel the increased rhythm of his heartbeat. She felt desire grow and expand within her. The demand of her mouth became as active as his own.

He slipped his hand beneath the thick sweater she wore and released the fastening of her bra. He pulled her across his lap, making her wholly aware of his arousal, and she felt the tender torture of his lips at her breasts, mouthing their swollen fullness with caressing appreciation, tightening over their hardening nipples with disturbing effect so that she gasped his name in an agony of pleasure.

Her arms about Teale's neck, she strained closer to him, shudder after shudder running through her awakened body and, in acknowledgement of her response, she felt the unsteady rise and fall of his chest. Caressingly, his hands slid the length of her, curved about her buttocks, stroked and kneaded. Slow, selective caresses set her pulses leaping, and a fierce, warm throb of sensation akin to pain flowed through her. She ached for complete fulfilment.

'Briony,' he muttered the words into the softness of her neck, 'come upstairs with me—now.' His caress had an increasing urgency, and at his words she trembled convulsively. Every bodily instinct urged her to agree to give him what he wanted, to take what she so sorely needed. It would be so easy to comply, to assuage the needs of their bodies. And, surely, once they had made love he would find he cared for her...

But Briony knew she was only deluding herself. He'd been brutally honest; for him, this wasn't love, merely a brief, sensual pleasure. For her, it could only mean future heartache. Mere physical fulfilment would leave her emotionally empty.

'No, Teale.' Despite his attempts to restrain her, she found the strength to struggle free of him, and stood up. 'I'm sorry, but I don't want it to be this way.' With trembling fingers, she straightened out her clothing.

''You want me,' he protested throatily. 'I know you do. You can't deny it.'

For long seconds, grey eyes battled with blue. She was the first to look away.

'No, I *can't* deny it. It would be hypocritical to try,' she said quietly. 'Like you, I'm only human. But *unlike* you, I wouldn't find a casual relationship acceptable, or satisfying.'

'Briony,' he groaned her name. He stood up, and for a moment she thought he was going to try and take her in his arms again, that he would try to persuade her otherwise. 'I thought we understood each other. We've discussed this so often. Art is a jealous mistress, any form of art, whether it be composing, painting, writing, whatever. I thought we were two of a kind, that we both wanted to be free to lead our own lives, free from entanglements. But that...'

'But that we'd be able to hop in and out of bed from time to time, whenever the urge took us,' she finished his sentence for him, her tone bitter.

Unbelievably, he grinned. 'I wouldn't have put it quite like that. But, yes. Oh, come on, Briony.' And now he did move towards her, but she retreated, putting the long sofa between them.

'No, Teale. You've been frank with me. Now I'm going to be perfectly frank with you. I wanted you just then. I've admitted it. I still want you and,' low-voiced, 'it hurts.' She saw him swallow and he moved restlessly.

'Briony...'

'No. Hear me out.' She faced him squarely, though it cost her an effort to do so. 'If I let you make love to me, exactly what you don't want would happen. I'd fall in love with you. That's the way I'm made. I honestly believe most women are made that way. I'd want to be with you all the time, to belong to you, to bear your children.' Her voice was husky with feeling and she knew her eyes were overbright with unshed tears. 'And I'd want the same commitment from you.'

He didn't answer her immediately. His dark, lean face was drawn into hard, expressionless planes, and she thought that she had angered him.

'I'd better go,' she said unhappily. She moved towards the door.

'No, wait.' All the tension seemed to have drained out of him, and he spoke wearily. 'I understand. No,' he contradicted himself. 'I don't *understand*. I don't think I'll ever understand women, but I *accept* that you mean what you say. I suppose I was hoping that being an artist would make you different.'

'In what way?' she puzzled, not sure if she should take offence. 'Because you think artists are more inclined to promiscuity? Anyway,' sarcastically, 'I thought you had strong views on that subject?'

'No,' he said harshly, 'I don't think artists are less moral than anyone else. Not even my worst enemy could accuse me of such a sweeping generalisation. And I don't believe what I'm suggesting *is* promiscuity. It would be a one-to-one relationship, as binding in its way as marriage. Even though we wouldn't be living under the same roof, there wouldn't be anyone else for me, if I had you. I'd expect it to be that way, too, for you. No, it's a question of realities. I thought *you'd* see them more clearly.'

'I'm afraid you'll have to explain.' Briony knew she should leave. Her heart was aching unbearably and there was a painful emptiness within her. She wanted to be alone to cry out her misery. But she also wanted desperately to understand this man. As though by understanding she could alter him, she mocked herself.

'Matthew paints red skies, all the time. Right?'

'Right,' she agreed dully, still not seeing the point of his argument.

'I'm trying to make an analogy with painting. *We* know skies aren't red, except for natural phenomena such as sunsets and so on. But Matthew lives in a world of his own, he doesn't acknowledge reality. That's always been one of his problems. So he paints his skies red, regardless. For him, skies *are* red.'

Briony nodded, following him thus far.

'You're different. *You* could colour a sky red simply because *you know* it's blue.'

She nodded again, though her attention was more for him than for his words, for the things about him that she loved.

'I'm not an artist,' Teale persevered. 'I colour things the way they really are. And I know that what you see, when you think of marriage to me, you see through rose-coloured spectacles. That's not the reality. You and I, we can never colour our skies red. The reality would be a grey hell.' Bitterly, 'Ask Charlene.'

That was the last straw.

'I don't *want* to ask Charlene!' No longer able to contain her feelings, Briony exploded suddenly, 'I'm *not* Charlene, I'm *me*! I'm different. How dare you lump me with her? How dare you tell me that I couldn't make marriage work? Because that *is* what you're telling me.' She knew her voice was shaking, knew to her shame that the tears so long held back were spilling over.

'Briony! Briony! Please don't cry. Oh, God! Look, love, I didn't mean to upset you.' He moved swiftly towards her and put his hands on her shoulders, but she resisted his efforts to pull her any closer. If he once did that, she might break down altogether. 'Of course I'm not saying marriage wouldn't work for *you*. I'm sure you'd make someone a splendid wife. Seeing you with Scott these past weeks tells me you'd also be a good mother. What I'm saying is, it wouldn't work for *me*. And you deserve something better.'

'And you think something better is an affair!' she choked.

'No! No!' He sighed exasperatedly. 'I can see now I was wrong to think that, wrong to suggest it. Oh, look, love, can't we forget this ever happened? I don't want to lose your friendship.' He looked anxiously into her face. 'Briony?'

'I don't know,' she said wearily. 'Things *can't* be unsaid, however much you might wish it. Things can never really be the same as they were before. Let me go, Teale.'

'Not yet. Not until you tell me...'

'Oh, don't be so damned selfish, Teale!' Anger at last came to her rescue, and she beat small, ineffectual fists against his chest. 'You want everything *your* way. You don't want love. You don't want a permanent relationship. But you still want me to go on coming here, no matter how much it hurts me.'

'Damn it!' He gave her an angry shake. 'Do you think *I'm* incapable of feeling hurt?'

'All that's hurting you is your pride—because I've turned you down.'

'Is *that* all you think it is?' His jaw tightened. 'I'll show you what hurt is.' There was passion and ruthlessness now in his dark face. 'Hurt is wanting what you can't have.' One of his arms ensnared her waist, while his free hand tangled itself in her hair, holding her head so that she could not evade his seeking lips, his kiss blazing into a consuming demand.

At the hardened thrust of his thighs against hers, Briony felt a quiver run over her and was furious with herself for reacting. But, as she parted her lips to protest, his probing tongue invaded them, his anger transformed into deep, driving hunger. Though she struggled, making little sounds of protest in her throat, he did not slacken the relentless onslaught on her mouth.

Gradually, Briony felt her will being sapped. Despite herself, her body curved against him, trying to achieve the maximum closeness. Her hands crept inside his shirt, traced the hard lines of his body, explored the roughness of hair that made a V down over the flat, muscular stomach.

He pulled her down on to the sofa, his hand brushing her skirt back over her thighs. The sudden movement made her breath catch in her throat as his hand moved upward, shaping her slowly, unhurriedly, sensuously, with an expertise that left her totally without resistance, until she was oblivious to everything but the wild desire she felt for him, the helpless agony of wanting. She longed for him to take her. She knew that if he swept her up in his arms now and carried her upstairs she would go unresistingly.

As he held her a little away from him, she looked into his eyes, hers all too revealing. She was dazed, flushed, mindless, trembling.

'Teale,' she murmured. 'Oh, Teale,' her breath sobbed in her throat.

'Briony?' he questioned her.

A storm of passion shook her, the thunderous call of her senses deafening her to everything else. Oblivious to right and wrong, to future heartache, she knew only that she loved him.

'Yes! I want you, Teale! Oh, love me!' she gasped. 'Please, please, love me!'

She was utterly devastated when he put her away from him and stood up.

'No, Briony!' His breathing was ragged, but his voice was harsh, determined.

'Why? Oh, Teale, why?' She held out an imploring hand but he turned his back on her and spoke into the glowing fire.

'You've already told me why. I'm not particularly proud of my behaviour just now. But I *do* have enough self-control to stop before things go too far.' The colour drained from Briony's face, making her eyes seem larger, a darker shade of blue. *She* had been the one lacking in self-control. 'I won't make love to you, Briony,' Teale went on, 'unless you can tell me—in cold blood—that it's what you want. That you're prepared to accept me on *my* terms. And somehow,' he said it heavily, 'I don't think you'll ever do that.'

He was right, of course. Though her body still ached and yearned for his, sanity now prevailed.

'I think it would be best,' she said, low-voiced, 'if we didn't see each other any more. I shan't come here again. Oh,' as he turned as if to protest, 'I'll finish the painting—if you still want it. I've done enough preparatory work now to be able to complete it in the studio.'

'Briony——' he began, but she held up a slender hand that trembled slightly.

'No, don't say any more. I think we've said all there is to say. Goodbye, Teale. I hope...' She had to pause to regain control of her voice, which had a tendency to crack under stress. 'I hope things work out well for you and little Scott.'

'I'll run you home.'

'No, please. If you'll just phone for a taxi...'

'Don't talk nonsense.' His tone was brusque. 'By the time you've waited for a taxi to come out from Gwinvercombe, I can have you home.'

Several times on the journey she had to brush a surreptitious hand across brimming eyes. She had been given just a brief view of the paradise she yearned for, and it made it all that much harder to accept that it could never be hers. But, for her, paradise signified perfection, and Teale's offer to her was flawed.

As the Rolls drew up outside the Blue Unicorn, Briony was ready, her seat-belt unfastened, to slide out of the car and make a swift getaway. But Teale's hard hand on her upper arm detained her. For a moment he did not speak, and her heart thudded violently against her ribcage. But she refused to hope. Just as well, she thought afterwards.

'I'm sorry, Briony. Sorry, I mean, that things turned out this way. I'd no idea you felt so strongly.' He hesitated, and Briony's nerves screamed for him to release her so that she could get away and seek the privacy she needed. She was still close to tears, tears she *would not* shed in front of him. 'I don't know how to put this without sounding presumptuous or conceited...'

'Then don't say *anything*,' she told him in low, urgent tones.

'But I must. Believe me, I never meant to hurt you, Briony. I thought we understood each other. But...' again he was hesitant, 'but it seems your feelings for me go deeper than...'

'Heavens!' She knew she sounded shrill and brittle, but at all costs she had to preserve some fragments of her shattered pride. 'Is *that* the impression I gave you?'

'Briony,' he interrupted her harshly, 'don't demean your feelings by denying them. You've no reason to feel ashamed of them. I'm the one to blame. I should have stayed away from you as soon as I realised... I should feel...'

'I don't think there's any point in holding a post-mortem.' In her turn, Briony interrupted. She succeeded in freeing herself as, momentarily, his grasp slackened. Then, lightly, she said, 'Don't lose any sleep over it, Teale. I certainly shan't,' she added mendaciously. 'I've survived worse things than this. Goodbye!'

He made no further protest, and from inside the darkened shop she watched his departure. It seemed a long time before the Rolls finally glided away. The sight of it moving out of sight seemed to release the tight control she had kept over herself and, muffling her sobs so as not to disturb Promilla, she made for the sanctuary of her room. Once there, she was able to let the tears flow freely.

'I don't know whether I *ought* to go away at Christmas and leave you all alone like this.' Promilla looked worried as she surveyed her friend the next morning. 'You look terrible,' she added with more truth than tact.

For all her efforts, Briony had been unable to obliterate the traces of her sleepless, tearful night and, when pressed, she had confided the cause of her unhappiness to her friend.

'Nonsense!' she said now. 'Of course you must go away. It's ten days yet, and I'll be perfectly all right by then. And I'll have Iseult.'

'If she comes! You've heard nothing.'

'Whether she comes or not,' Briony said firmly, '*You* are going to see your great-aunt and that's that!'

A few days after the auction sale, the month of November dragged itself into a dreary close, the worsening weather adding to Briony's despondency. Long-range forecasts predicted a harsh winter ahead. Iseult had not written again. Briony had telephoned Jean-Luc's Paris office several times, but without success, though she'd left messages asking Jean-Luc to return her call. Promilla had gone up to London again to make final arrangements with Ramamurthie Pati for her trip to Karachi. Briony was alone. The shop was closed for the night.

Normally, under such circumstances, she would have taken the opportunity to go up to the studio and do some painting. But the only work she had in hand at present was that of the manor house, and she couldn't bear to look at it. She'd eaten a very frugal evening meal, sharing most of it with the cats—her appetite seemed to have disappeared—and was just clearing away her solitary cup and plate when the doorbell rang. She was tempted not to answer its summons, for there was no one she wanted to see. It was probably carol singers anyway, she thought. They started coming earlier and earlier every year, and she certainly wasn't in a festive mood.

Whoever it was didn't intend to go away. The bell continued to ring, and then the letter flap was rattled violently. Briony did something foreign to her nature—she swore. She started for the door, promising herself she would give the persistent intruders a piece of her mind.

It wasn't Christmas carollers. Her stomach turned with a sickening rush. It was Teale who stood framed in the doorway against the light of a street-lamp. His raincoat

was damp and his hair slicked wetly about his head. Icy
rain fell steadily, splashing into already existing puddles,
streaming from overworked gutterings, running in rivu-
lets down the steep High Street. Taken aback, the words
she'd intended to say frozen on her lips, Briony stood
immobilised.

'Well, can I come in?' Teale enquired impatiently. 'It's
pouring cats and dogs out here!'

Still wordless, reluctantly she stood aside, and he
strode past her, bringing a rush of cold air with him.
Only then did she realise that he carried a large cardboard box.

'Your goods from the auction,' he explained as he
preceded her through the kitchen and into the living-
room. 'They were delivered with mine.'

Normally, the arrival of her purchases would have excited Briony's enthusiasm. Normally, she couldn't wait
to unpack and see if the items were as choice as they'd
seemed in the auction room. Not this time.

'I'm sorry you've been put to the trouble of bringing
them round,' said Briony stiffly. She stood watching him
with dispirited eyes as he deposited his load on a chair,
then straightened and turned to face her.

'It was no trouble. Besides, I wanted to see you.'

'Oh!' she said unhelpfully. She couldn't think *why* he
should want to see her. She remained standing. She
wasn't going to ask him to sit down, either. She didn't
want him to stay.

'Sally had her pups the night before last. I wondered—when they're old enough to leave her—whether
you'd like to have one?'

As a constant reminder of you? she thought painfully.
She shook her head. 'I don't think that would be a very
good idea.'

'I thought you said you'd like a dog. Or is it,' ironically, 'because the offer comes from me?' He'd shown this uncanny knack of reading her mind before.

'No,' she denied. 'I just don't have time—with the shop and everything—to housetrain a pup.'

'Suppose I were to train it before I handed it over?'

Briony hesitated. She had fallen in love with Sally, and she would dearly have liked one of the Springer spaniel's pups. But again she shook her head.

'No. Thank you very much all the same. And thank you for bringing these over.' She indicated the box. 'Promilla's been dying to see what I bought.' She was patently waiting for him to leave, and Teale made as if to do so. But then he stopped.

'Is Promilla in?'

She could have said yes, but she disliked lies. She shook her head.

'Then perhaps we could talk?'

'I don't think...'

'Oh, look, Briony,' his tone was coaxing, 'this is ridiculous, isn't it?' For an instant, a sparkle of hope and love shone in her blue eyes, but his next words extinguished it. 'We're both of us adults. We're responsible to no one else. We want each other. At least, *I* haven't stopped wanting *you*.' Her treacherous heart leaped at the admission, and colour flamed into her cheeks. 'What's the point in denying ourselves the satisfaction we can bring each other?' Briony began to shake her head again, but Teale asked, 'Can't we at least sit down and discuss it in a civilised fashion?'

'We've already discussed it,' she told him wearily, 'the other night. Nothing's changed since then.'

'What is it with you?' he demanded. 'Are you afraid?'

'I'm *not* afraid,' she told him, her voice trembling with pain. 'Would I be holding out for marriage if I were afraid of it? Not that it's any of your business. But I won't have you implying... I *told* you my reasons. Now, will you please go?' Briony knew she was starting a headache. She had all the classic symptoms: the frontal pain, the aching neck, the feeling of nausea.

'I want you, but I won't be blackmailed into marriage,' he warned.

Briony exploded with anger.

'Have I asked you to marry me?' she demanded. 'All I've done is to ask you to go away, told you I'm not interested in your—your "proposition". I *know* marriage wouldn't suit *you*, you've made that plain enough. Besides, you're much too concerned about your selfish physical needs to see the beauty and fulfilment that come from loving someone in every possible way. Marriage *is* beautiful.' Her voice broke on the words and her head throbbed more painfully than before.

'So is physical love!' he retorted. 'If you'd only let me show you...' And, as she retreated a step or two, 'Damn you, Briony!' He reached her in a couple of long strides. His hands were twin vises on her shoulders. 'I *will* show you! How can you deny us both this?' His descending mouth was inescapable. There was time for only one quick protesting breath before his lips were bruising hers. Then his arms encircled her, crushing her against his chest, constricting her lungs so that she felt faint and dizzy.

He went on kissing her with an aching need, while his hands slid down her spine, forcing her to arch her body towards him. Hard, muscular thighs forced intimate pressure upon her and she trembled beneath his onslaught. Passion leapt between them. Murmuring incoherently, Briony began to return his kisses. But Teale's hunger seemed unappeased by her feverish response, and a roughness in his touch spoke of feelings getting beyond control.

He pushed her down on to the couch, the imprisoning weight and warmth of his body a potent intoxicant. Slowly, sensually, his long sensitive fingers explored the warm curves of her body, coaxing reactions from her that sent shock-waves through her so that she was frantic with her need of him. He was trembling against her and she was aware of the thrusting demand of his masculinity. She wanted him as much as he wanted her. Yet something held her back from asking him to make love to her.

When at last he released her mouth, relaxing his hold, she lay weakly in his arms, too drained and defenceless to attempt to break free. Her eyes were pleading as she looked up at him, pleading for his love, his understanding. But his were cold steel, hard, emotionless.

'Do you realise now something of what you're denying us?' he demanded. 'Oh, don't worry, Briony,' he bit out as she parted her lips to speak, 'I'm not going to force you. In fact, I'm leaving now, unless...' His expression was still hard, as he went on, 'unless you're going to ask me to stay?'

Weakly, she shook her head. She wouldn't compromise her beliefs.

'Very well!' He released her completely, stood up and strode towards the door.

Forced to follow him in order to lock up, Briony held her sobs strangled in her throat. Dignity begged her not to let him see her in tears. Without another glance or another word, Teale vanished into the cold, wet night. Then there was only pain.

CHAPTER EIGHT

'WHEN are you going to finish the painting of Teale's house?' Rhoda asked two or three weeks later in a lull between serving customers. 'I've just seen it standing with its face to the wall. Is there something wrong with it?'

Briony shrugged. 'No, there's nothing wrong. I've just gone off it for the time being.' It was true. The painting had been going very well. She had imbued her work with the love she felt for the house, but more especially for its owner. And it was the first time she could remember leaving a picture unfinished. Always, even when a painting was going badly, she would struggle to pull it together, maintaining that you could learn even from your mistakes.

'Or you've gone off my brother—for the time being?' Rhoda probed shrewdly. 'You haven't been seeing him lately, have you? And he hasn't mentioned your name for some while.'

Briony looked pensively at her, wondering whether to confide in Teale's sister. She was missing having Promilla to talk to. Her friend had left ten days ago for Karachi. But no, she decided, she didn't know Rhoda well enough. Besides, the other woman's loyalty to her brother might prompt her to take up cudgels in his defence.

'Teale and I *have* had a disagreement,' she admitted at last.

'Well, Christmas is the season of goodwill,' Rhoda said cheerfully. 'I'm sure you'll make it up then. I did warn you he's a bear when he's in the middle of a book. I should just let him get it out of his system if I were you.' A little later, she asked, 'What are you doing for the two days?'

'Oh, nothing special. I think Christmas is an over-rated occasion. The true meaning of it has been swamped in commercialism.'

Rhoda looked at her speculatively.

'That doesn't sound like you, Briony. I'd have put you down as a traditionalist, even a sentimentalist. I know what it is!' she exclaimed. 'You're putting on a brave face, aren't you, because you're going to be on your own?' She seemed struck by a sudden thought. 'Why not spend Christmas at the cottage with us? You know Libby, and you could meet the rest of the children. They'll be home till the New Year. Matthew and I would love to have you.'

'Oh, no!' Briony protested hastily. 'I mean,' she faltered, 'thank you, but Christmas is a family time. I wouldn't dream of intruding. Besides,' as if it were the clincher, 'I couldn't leave the cats.'

But Rhoda was not that easily put off.

'Bring them with you. We've no indoor pets to upset them. They'd soon settle down.'

'Oh, dear,' Briony sighed. 'It's very kind of you. You're making it very difficult to refuse. But look, Rhoda, I'll have to be perfectly honest with you. You're bound to want Teale and little Scott with you over the holiday, and I just don't want to see Teale again—ever. Don't ask me why, please,' she begged.

'I see,' Rhoda said slowly. 'I'm sorry. I didn't realise it was that serious. I thought things were going well be-tween you two nowadays. You seemed to be so ideal for him. You have your own interests. You understand his need to write, the way he needs to shut himself off sometimes.'

Briony winced. Rhoda's words were so close to the arguments Teale himself had put forward. She was glad when the arrival of several customers put an end to their conversation.

'But I will finish the painting,' she promised.

When Bob Daish had callously broken off their engagement, following the death of Briony's father, the pain of his defection had eased to a dull ache within a very short time. But although there had never been any real relationship between her and Teale, the hurt of not seeing him, of knowing he could never be hers, was as tormentingly real, weeks after their last encounter, as it had ever been.

Briony had spent Christmas alone, after all. Jean-Luc had finally telephoned, but only to tell her that Iseult was promised to his parents in Provence for the whole of the school holidays, but that she would contact Briony in the New Year.

In the event, apart from her aching heart, the solitary holiday hadn't proved to be too much of an ordeal. Briony had always possessed great reserves of self-sufficiency. She watched and enjoyed the seasonal programmes on television, caught up on her reading and determinedly made herself finish the painting of the manor house. The sooner it was finished, the sooner she could put the house and its owner out of her mind. Rhoda could deliver it to her brother. There would be no reason then for Briony to see him again.

The Blue Unicorn was open for the only three working days between Christmas and the New Year, though Briony did not expect much trade. After the Christmas expenditure, there would be little money to spare for arts and crafts, and in any case most people would be travelling to the big towns for the sales. The weather was growing progressively colder and since Christmas Eve spasmodic snowfalls had whitened the High Street.

'Don't bother to come in next week,' Briony had told Rhoda when they'd closed on Christmas Eve. 'You don't want to drive over here in this weather. I can manage for three days.'

But Rhoda had turned up, despite deteriorating conditions.

'I came on the bus,' she said when Briony remonstrated with her. 'Besides, I wanted to see if you were all right. I kept thinking about you over the holiday, here all on your own.' She went on, 'You could have come to us, as it turned out. Teale had a telephone call from his ex-mother-in-law on Christmas morning. Charlene's worse. And with no trains running he had to drive up to London. One thing I'm determined on, if he's not back by New Year's Eve, you're seeing the New Year in with us. Next year is going to be a big one for Matthew, with his exhibition coming up, and it's all owing to you. We must celebrate.'

'I'd like that,' Briony admitted.

'Have you heard from Promilla at all?' Rhoda asked as they took down Christmas decorations and renewed the counter and window displays.

'There was a letter in this morning's post.' Briony fished it out of her skirt pocket and handed it to Rhoda. 'It must have got held up with all the extra mail. She had a very warm welcome from her great-aunt. You'll see she also speaks glowingly of the Patis' son. "Rama", she calls him. They seem to be getting on very well. I wouldn't be at all surprised to see a romance develop there.'

'How would it affect *you* if it did?' Rhoda asked as she returned the letter. 'If Promilla were to get married, and to a Londoner?'

Briony had been thinking about that herself since the letter had arrived.

'I'd miss Prom, of course,' she said sadly. 'But I'd like to see her happily married. I think that's what she's always wanted. She loves children and she's a very motherly person. I could just about afford to buy her out, I suppose. Or we might decide to sell up.' She shrugged a little despondently. 'I'd be sorry in a way. I like Devon enormously, but I think maybe the time's come for me to move on.'

'You wouldn't be running away from that brother of mine by any chance?'

'Hardly "running away"!' Briony said wryly. 'He's not exactly "chasing" me, is he?' Her words revealed more to the other woman than she realised. 'But yes, I think it might be a good idea to get right away.'

'I know this is all speculation as yet,' Rhoda said slowly, 'but I do like to plan ahead. If Promilla *were* by any chance to get married, I'd like to come in with you—that's if you did decide to stay here. But perhaps you wouldn't care to have a new partner?'

'Oh, but I would!' Briony smiled warmly at her. 'I can't think of anything I'd like more.' Then her smile faded. 'If I were to stay.'

'Well,' Rhoda said, 'whatever happens, don't decide anything in a hurry. You never know, things might work out between you and Teale yet.'

Briony wished she could share Rhoda's optimism.

'So you're definitely coming tonight?' Rhoda pressed Briony at closing time on New Year's Eve.

'Yes, please, if you're sure Teale won't...'

'We haven't heard a word from him, neither has Mrs Barrett. I think you're safe enough.' Rhoda sighed. 'But I do wish Teale would come to his senses.' Under pressure, Briony had told Teale's sister of his determination never to marry again. 'You're so *right* for him.'

'Nothing formal, but definitely party-wear,' had been Rhoda's parting instructions. Thoughtfully, Briony surveyed her wardrobe. Bearing in mind that whatever she wore must be covered by warm outer clothing for the drive to the cottage, she settled on a stylish but comfortable turquoise-blue trouser suit in a silky material that clung lovingly to her slender figure and shimmered with the wearer's every move. Matching shoes went in a bag, to be donned on arrival. Her hair had grown considerably in the last few months, and she brushed her copper curls vigorously, tying them back at the nape of her neck with a broad black velvet ribbon. In the daytime she wore very little make-up, but for evening she applied a smooth, transparent film of foundation. Blue shadow emphasised the colour of her eyes and complemented her outfit. A blue silk purse in an oriental fabric completed the ensemble.

Briony had never been vain, but she was moderately satisfied with her appearance. Ruefully, she caught herself thinking that, if Teale were to have been present, she would have agonised far more over what to wear. But then, she reminded herself, if he'd been there, *she* wouldn't be going.

She checked that the cats had plenty of food and water and clean litter, then locked up carefully. The car, which had been standing idle for several days, needed a little persuasion to start, but before long she was on the road out of Gwinvercombe. She drove cautiously, for the steep, narrow lanes were coated with that day's fall of snow, which traffic had packed into a hard surface that glistened diamondlike in the moonlight. The sky held a promise of more snow still to come.

There were one or two cars parked outside the cottage. None of them, she was relieved to see, was a silver Rolls-Royce. If it had been, she would have turned straight round and driven home.

Matthew opened the door to her and she marvelled anew at what the prospects of success had done for his appearance and self-confidence.

'Rhoda's in the kitchen performing miracles,' he informed her. 'Come in and I'll introduce you to some of our friends.'

Not surprisingly, many of these were from the arts world, and Briony found no shortage of shared interests or topics for conversation. But it seemed the evening was not to be purely an intellectual one. Rhoda's hand-tufted rugs had been rolled back from the gleaming polished floors to allow for dancing, and there were team games, some of them extremely energetic. Riding pick-a-back on a large jolly giant of a man, a laughing and extremely flushed Briony found herself suddenly face to face with the last person she had expected to see. She felt as if her heart had stopped completely in that instant of disbelief. Unnoticed by anyone, Teale had arrived and stood in the doorway towards which they were careering.

As he stepped further into the room, she saw that he was not dressed for a party. Over his thick sweater and trousers he wore a heavy sheepskin driving coat. In the harshness of the bright overhead light, his face looked pale and strained, his dark eyes hollowed by fatigue. Flakes of snow spangled his black hair, imitating a sprinkling of the grey its raven sheen did not in reality possess.

His dark eyes had not yet left her face, and her own grew large with pain and confusion as she could not decide whether she were glad or sorry to see him again.

'Teale,' she murmured his name and saw his head dip in polite acknowledgement. She felt ridiculous, still perched on the large man's back, and to her relief he let her slide to the ground as the game was postponed in honour of Teale's arrival.

'We weren't expecting you back tonight, and in such awful weather!' Rhoda exclaimed and her anxious glance at Briony did not escape Teale's attention. Briony saw his lips tighten.

'So it would seem.'

'But you're very welcome,' his sister went on hastily. 'Give me your coat. Matthew, get Teale a drink.'

Briony half expected Teale to say he wasn't staying, but he shrugged off his coat, accepted the glass his brother-in-law handed him and sank on to the large sofa which had been pushed into a corner of the room. He smiled up at his sister, though the smile was a weary one.

'It's good to be home. I suddenly felt I couldn't stand London another minute. Whatever the weather, I decided I'd try and get through.'

Teale's arrival seemed to put an end to the noisy, riotous fun, or maybe the guests had been tired anyway. Rhoda announced that supper would now be served, and soon people were seated on chairs or on the floor with loaded plates filled from the generous buffet.

Briony had contrived to find a seat where Teale's compelling gaze could not find her, but she was close enough to be able to hear his low-voiced conversation with his sister and to gather that his ex-wife had died over the Christmas holiday. She felt saddened, as she would be by the news of anyone's death, and particularly at such a time of year, and she wondered just how much Teale was affected by it. Did he regret the last few years of separation now that there was no chance of a reconciliation?

She was relieved when the large man, whose name she had discovered was Ivor, drew her into an animated discussion on Impressionist art. It was impossible to forget Teale's presence, but at least she need not let him see how much it disturbed her; when the dancing recommenced she willingly let Ivor lead her on to the floor.

As the only unpartnered woman at the party, she was much in demand among the Rawlinsons' unattached male friends, and she danced every dance. She was aware of Teale dancing, too. Sometimes the movement brought him and his partner so close that her arm brushed against his in passing, but she steadfastly avoided meeting his eyes. She was aware of a strange kind of tension whenever he was near, as though some tangible sensation passed between them. But it could only be in her own imagination, she told herself.

She had not expected that he would ask her to dance, and when he did it was impossible to refuse under the eyes of the other guests. She had to breathe in deeply to steady her trembling voice as she accepted. She was desperately afraid that any physical contact with him would destroy the fragile defences she had erected.

It was growing late and most couples were intimately entwined. Teale took her in a similarly close hold, her hand held to the warmth of his chest so that she could feel the steady heartbeat beneath the rough wool of his sweater. The male scent of him was in her nostrils, intoxicating her senses, and it was an exquisite agony to feel the pressure of his hard body against hers. He did not speak at first, though his mouth was near enough to her ear for him to have done so had he wished. The music was a slow, sultry number, the vocalisation husky, the words of the song spoke of tender love, of passion. The skilful pressure of Teale's legs guided her around the floor. His hand, placed firmly at the base of her spine, prevented her easing away from him.

'Did you spend Christmas here, too?'

She could sense that he was looking down at her, but she kept her eyes firmly fixed on the beige wool of his sweater.

'No.' Her voice was so low that he had to incline his head to hear her and she felt a strand of his hair brush her temple.

'Ah! Of course! I forgot. You were expecting someone?' He was patently waiting for a detailed reply, but all he received was a muffled 'yes'.

'Was it an enjoyable Christmas?'

'Yes, thank you.' She must ask Rhoda not to reveal that she'd spent it alone.

He tried to see into her face

'You're very monosyllabic tonight. Are you still angry with me?'

'No!' She tried to sound surprised, indifferent.

She must have succeeded, for there was a note of chagrin in his voice as he said, 'And you haven't missed me either, I take it?'

'Christmas is a busy time,' she said evasively. 'Even more so with Promilla away.'

There was a long silence and she began to think he had abandoned any attempts at conversation. The dance seemed never-ending. She risked a glance at her wristwatch and wondered how soon she could decently leave the party. It was almost midnight. She would wait for the New Year toasts, she decided, then bid Rhoda a discreet farewell. With luck, she could slip away without advertising her departure.

At last their dance ended, but somehow the deprivation of his nearness was worse than the disturbing closeness.

At five minutes to twelve Matthew switched on the radio so that Big Ben's midnight chimes would be heard; and they stood around, charged glasses in hand. As the last chime faded away there began a round of handshaking and kissing. Briony dreaded the moment when she would encounter Teale, and when she did so she held out her hand, hoping he would take the hint.

He clasped her hand, but he used it to draw her closer, and she made the mistake of meeting his eyes. There was the electrifying sensation of something linking, tightening, an intolerable tension that quivered between them.

'Why so formal, Briony?' he said mockingly and then she was in his arms, held in an iron-hard embrace. Her blood throbbed in urgent pulses as his lips sought and claimed hers.

It was no token kiss. One strong arm about her waist prevented her from moving. His free hand curved the shape of her cheek, the fingertips caressing the sensitive

spot behind her ear. As the kiss grew in intensity, so did
the pressure of his body against hers, and Briony was
left in no doubt that he was aroused. Her body leapt
with answering erotic sensation and, in spite of everything, she thrilled to the knowledge that she could still
have this effect on him.

A rousing cheer from the other guests alerted her to
the fact that their kiss had gone on far too long. Flushing,
she struggled free, heart still thudding wildly. She saw
Rhoda's eyes upon her, speculative and approving, and
from a momentary exaltation of spirits Briony plum-
meted to despair. Only *she* knew how little that kiss had
meant to Teale in terms of affection. It had been purely
physical, a passing moment of lust excited by good food,
drink and the occasion. As he moved on to kiss someone
else, she gained Rhoda's side.

'Will you excuse me if I go now?' She was aware that
her voice was tremulous. 'I don't want to be too late
driving back.'

'Briony,' Rhoda began, 'why don't you...?'

'No one's going to be driving anywhere,' one of the
other guests interrupted. 'I've just been outside to look
at the weather.' He made a general announcement. 'We
seem to be snowed in, folks.'

There was a buzz of exclamation and everyone hurried
to the door to verify the truth of his statement. Around
the cottage, the snow lay not in inches but at least a foot
in depth. The guests' cars, including Briony's, all wore
a thick coating. Snow still fell, whirled into blizzardlike
proportions by a strong chill wind.

'There'll be heavy drifting on the roads,' someone said.

'And it's freezing hard,' said another, 'the roads will
be like a skating rink.'

'Visibility will be poor,' a third added.

'You'll all have to stay overnight,' Rhoda decided. 'It
won't be very comfortable, I'm afraid. With all the kids
home for the holiday, we only have one spare bedroom,

and Mary and John have already bagged that.' She indicated an elderly couple who had travelled some distance for the party.

'There's plenty of rooms up at my place,' Teale broke in, 'if you're willing to make up the beds yourselves.'

Briony had too much sense to protest that she would try to get home. She knew only too well how dangerous the narrow, high-banked lanes around Gwinvercombe could be in this kind of weather. But she looked anxiously at Rhoda, hoping the other woman would suggest some way she could remain at the cottage. Even an armchair would suffice.

Rhoda, however, seemed not to notice Briony's despairing glance as she busied herself organising gumboots for those who had none. Perhaps she didn't want the trouble of an extra overnight guest.

Five minutes later, Briony found herself one of a noisy party who laughed, whooped and joked as they slipped and slithered over the already hardening surface on the long trek up to the big house. Only Briony was silent, dreading the hours that must be spent under Teale's roof.

On arrival at the manor they all trooped into the large kitchen where the women set to, making hot drinks to thaw everyone out after the cold traipse through the snow, which in places had been knee-deep. No one seemed to be in any hurry to retire. In fact, the gathering in the kitchen looked like developing into another party. They might as well have stayed at Rhoda's until first light, Briony thought miserably, then she would have been spared this ordeal.

She'd believed herself unnoticed as she huddled in a corner of the kitchen, her hands clasped for comfort around the hot mug of coffee—the chill she felt was more than that caused by the weather—but Teale came towards her.

'This lot look set in for the night,' he said, confirming her own thoughts. 'But *you* look tired. Would you like me to show you your room?'

'If you'll just tell me which one it is, I'll find my own way,' she said quickly. 'There's no need for you to leave your guests.'

'They're not mine!' His tone was wry. 'They're all Rhoda's friends. They won't miss *me*.' A hand under her elbow, he steered her out of the kitchen and into the front hall. 'I suppose Rhoda didn't think to lend you any nightclothes?' And, as she shook her head, 'I'd better find you something to wear. The central heating will have gone off hours ago.' He paused at the door of what Briony knew to be his room. 'Come in and I'll see what I can find.'

'I'll wait for you here,' she told him and saw the sudden awareness that lit his eyes.

'Why, Briony,' he murmured putting a finger under her chin, 'I do believe you're afraid of me.' She *was* afraid, but not only of him, of what he might say or do, but also of her own reactions to him. 'Little coward!' It was said affectionately. 'Come on in.' He gave her hand a tug and the irresistible need to be near him carried her into his room and the door closed behind them.

The light was switched on, illuminating his dark head and broad shoulders as he rummaged in a drawer.

'Will this do you?' He turned and held out a pyjama jacket. 'You can have the trousers as well, if you like, but I doubt you'd be able to keep them up.' His voice was suddenly husky as he moved back towards her, his eyes assessing her. 'You're such a little slip of a thing.'

'N-no, the jacket will do.' Briony held out her hand for the garment, but he kept hold of it so that it formed a link between them.

'I've been doing a hell of a lot of thinking while I've been away, Briony. There was plenty of time for thinking, sitting up all night and every night with Charlene.'

'I heard you tell Rhoda that she... I'm sorry, Teale.'

He nodded, accepting her sympathy. 'It isn't easy to watch someone you once believed you loved dying. But it made me realise something...' He paused, searched for words, and Briony found herself watching him with a painful intensity.

'It made me realise just how short life is,' he went on, 'and how much more there is to life than I've had out of it so far. It's true I have a lot more than some people. I'm a moderately successful man. I work at a profession I enjoy. I own this beautiful old house. I earn enough to keep myself in comfort for the rest of my life. But these are all material things, and I began to ask myself what else I had. Who is there really to care what becomes of me?'

'There's Rhoda and little Scott,' Briony said. 'Twins are always very close, and you have your son.' Whereas *I* have no one, she thought, not even my daughter, really. Nervous flutterings assailed her stomach. Her mouth was suddenly dry. She wanted him to go on, yet feared what he might say. She wanted him to tell her that his sister and his son were not enough, that he needed *her*, too. But suppose it was still only physical assuagement that he asked of her?

'Briony!' A tug of the pyjama jacket eliminated the distance between them. The jacket fell unheeded to the ground as long fingers dug almost painfully into her shoulders. 'I found myself thinking, suppose anything were to happen to *you*, as it happened to Charlene.' Thickly, he muttered, 'Do you still care for me, Briony?'

There was no point in denying that she *had* cared for him. Her behaviour at their last meeting had given that away. She stared up into unfathomable dark eyes. She did care for him still, oh, so much! But if she admitted it...

'Teale, I...'

'I told Rhoda I *had* to get back. It was true that I hate London and that I'd just experienced the most depressing few days I can ever remember. But I had other reasons for wanting to be at home. I wanted to come back to *you*, Briony.'

She drew in a quick, silent breath, her heart leaping. But she wouldn't make assumptions, would not let herself rejoice prematurely. There had been no commitment so far in what he'd said.

'I drove over to Gwinvercombe first, to the Blue Unicorn. When you weren't there, I hoped you might be at Rhoda's. Then, when I walked into that room and saw you with Ivor, for a moment I thought . . .' He drew her against the hard muscles of his chest, and a shiver of excruciating ecstasy quivered through her. 'I think,' muttered Teale, 'that's the first time in my life I've ever experienced blind, savage jealousy.' His hands moulded her closer to his hard male outline, and Briony felt his warm breath against her hair. 'I didn't realise till then that I'd come to think of you as mine. I still want you, Briony. God knows how I want you!' The masculine hardness against her left her in no doubt that he meant what he said.

But at his words she shivered. She felt she knew what he would say next. She ought to make an effort to break away from him, now, because the shock-waves of physical contact with him had undermined her resolve and she might very easily succumb if he tried to make love to her.

'Briony, the way you acted when we were last together made me almost certain that you loved me. Darling, won't you tell me? Put me out of this agony?'

For a moment she strained away, her hands pressed to his chest, struggling to deny the wild beat of her heart. But his hand curled around the back of her neck and he bent his head, murmuring muffled endearments against the thickness of her coppery hair. Her world spun crazily and Briony scarcely knew any longer what was right or wrong. All she knew was that her head whirled with his nearness. She could feel the acceleration of his breathing and felt him shudder as she yielded to his embrace, winding her arms about the muscular strength of his neck ...

She did not deny him as he kissed her with commanding strength and passion, his mouth buried hungrily in hers, deepening and deepening the kiss until she clung to him, limp with longing. Then his lips moved on to roam the hollows of her throat, while with one hand he sought for the fastenings at the back of the silky suit she wore. She felt the zip yield part-way to him, just enough to allow him to slip the bodice from her shoulders, allowing his hand to seek for and find her breasts. His exploring fingers paused and she felt him shudder as he discovered the peaks aroused by the magnetic chemistry of his hands.

'You want me, Briony,' he said positively, his mouth following the trail his lips had blazed. 'You want me. You can't deny it.'

'Yes, I want you.' She *couldn't* deny it, but it was reckless to admit it. Never had she been so conscious of her own feminine vulnerability as his caresses intensified.

'Love me, Briony,' he urged. 'Stay with me tonight. I need you. Let's begin the New Year together. Say yes, darling, please.'

She moaned as his hands, sensually exploring and masterful, began to slide the rest of the garment down over her hips, his touch kindling erotic fires wherever it brushed her skin. Shivers of desire cascaded down her spine.

'I love you, Teale,' she whispered. She ached with longing. 'I love you.'

He lifted his dark head and his eyes, full of ardent fire, studied her face.

'You see!' A complacent smile curved the sensual lines of his mouth, crinkling the corners of his eyes, and as always her heart performed crazy somersaults. 'I so nearly let you get away from me. But never again.' He began to draw her across the room towards the bed.

'But Teale...' He still hadn't said...

'No buts, my love.' His mouth descended again, cutting off her protests, his kiss sweetly possessive; she was unable to deny him, her lips moving lovingly under his. She seemed to have no will-power to refuse him whatever he wanted. The edge of the bed was behind her knees and they were sinking down on to it. In a moment, she would be lost. But it didn't seem so dreadful a fate, after all, when she compared it with the empty days without him.

'Mr Munro! Mr Munro! Is that you in there?'

There was an urgent knocking on the bedroom door, and Briony recognised Mrs Barrett's voice, raised in urgent summons.

Teale swore beneath his breath.

'Stay there,' he whispered, then called, 'I'm coming, Mrs Barrett. What is it?' He opened the door a fraction, sliding through it so that his housekeeper could not see right into the room. But Briony could overhear their conversation.

'Oh, it *is* you, Mr Munro. Such a relief! I heard all this noise going on downstairs. It woke little Scott, too. I wasn't expecting you back and I dared not go down to see, in case it was burglars.'

'My apologies, Mrs Barrett. I was forced to offer overnight accommodation to some of my sister's friends, because of the bad weather. I'm sorry if they've woken you. I'll go down and shut them up.' His voice receded.

With his departure, Briony shivered. The room was cold, but the shiver was not entirely due to that. The interruption had restored her to a much-needed sense of sanity. She had been on the point of forsaking her principles and letting Teale make love to her with no other commitment than that of mutual physical attraction. Still trembling, she adjusted the trouser suit. She wished she knew which room Teale intended to allocate her, so that she could slip away before he returned. As it was, she must wait and ask him. But, however much he tried, she resolved, she would not let him coax her back into her former pliancy.

The door, left ajar, opened wider and her throat contracted as she waited for Teale to reappear, afraid he would refuse to accept her decision. But it was little Scott who stood in the doorway.

'Daddy?' Then, as his eyes adjusted to the light, 'Oh good, it's you, Briony!' He ran to her and flung himself into her arms. 'You *have* come to share my daddy's bed.'

It was high time someone explained certain things to him, Briony thought.

'No, darling.' She pulled him on to her knee and cuddled the small form. 'Daddy and I were only talking. I'm going to my own room in a minute.'

'But you *are* staying here?'

'Just for tonight, because of the snow.'

'Oh!' Scott's face fell. 'I thought you'd decided to come and be my new mummy.'

'Not tonight, perhaps, but soon,' said a third voice, joining in their conversation. Teale stood in the doorway, smiling at them. He moved towards the bed and put a caressing hand on Briony's dishevelled hair. 'I don't believe I actually got around to asking you to marry me, did I, my love?'

Briony stared at him. She swallowed.

'Not exactly, no.' She wondered if her ears were playing her false. But it was not in her ears that she felt the sharp throb of response to his words.

'Remind me later,' he said softly, then, 'But first we'd better put this young man back to bed.'

'Don't want to go back to my room,' Scott announced. 'I want to sleep with Auntie Briony.' The determined set of his small mouth promised trouble if it was denied.

Teale groaned and Briony blushed as she met his eyes.

'All right,' Teale sighed. And to Briony, he said, 'I'll show you your room. Curse Rhoda's noisy friends,' he muttered *sotto voce*.

With Scott tucked into the spare-room bed Briony was to occupy, Teale drew Briony to the door and into his arms for a long, lingering kiss that reawoke desires that could not now be assuaged. Over her shoulder, he glanced at his son.

'I wish that were me,' he growled, his body hard with longing against hers. 'But there's always tomorrow, and then I'll make sure we're not disturbed.'

CHAPTER NINE

CAREFULLY, so as not to disturb Scott who was already asleep, Briony slid into bed. She was tired, but it was impossible to sleep. Yet it was even more impossible to believe she was awake. She felt she might yet regain consciousness, only to find that the last half-hour or so had been a dream.

She wished Teale's lovemaking had not been interrupted. But, if he'd meant what he said, she needed this time apart from him to collect her thoughts. There were aspects of her past about which he knew nothing, to which she must confess. In a way, she regretted that she had not taken Promilla's advice and told him earlier about Jean-Luc and Iseult. But she still believed she would have been presuming an interest in her personal life that he had not felt at that time.

'Wake up, Briony! Wake up!' She must have slept finally, for Scott had great difficulty in rousing her. 'Daddy said I must wish you a happy New Year.'

'Happy New Year, darling.' She kissed the end of his nose. And it *was* going to be a happy one, she thought exultantly, perhaps the happiest of her whole life. 'What time is it, for goodness' sake?' It felt like the middle of the night. But a glance at the wristwatch which she hadn't removed showed her it was gone ten o'clock.

'Everybody's having breakfast,' Scott told her.

'Then you scoot and have yours while I wash and dress. I'll be down in a moment.'

'Silly,' he said scornfully, 'I had mine with Daddy, hours ago.' But obediently he made for the door.

She had only last night's trouser suit to put on, but fortunately the material was of the sort that did not crease, and her face, glowing with the anticipation of seeing Teale again, needed no cosmetics.

Downstairs, the house seemed to be full of people, eating, drinking endless cups of coffee, talking and laughing. There had been a snow-clearing party before breakfast, and all the cars, including Briony's were now parked in the rear courtyard of the manor house.

With the memory of last night still vividly in her mind, Briony found it difficult to meet Teale's gaze, but once she did the expression in his eyes convinced her that none of it had been a dream, not even his proposal.

'I can't wait to get rid of this lot,' he murmured, 'so I can have you to myself.'

'But I can't stay.' Dismayed, she remembered. 'I have to get home to feed the cats.' Anxiously, 'Has it snowed much more? Will I be able to get through this morning?'

'The roads should be passable. In any case, I have snow chains on the Rolls. *I'll* get you back to Gwinvercombe.' His eyes gleamed wickedly and Briony blushed as he said, 'In fact, that will suit my purpose even better. There'll be no one *there* to interrupt us.'

To Briony, longing to be alone with Teale, Rhoda's friends seemed to take an unconscionably long time departing. But at last the final car had been waved on its way.

'Thank God for that!' Teale's words revealed that he had shared her impatience.

'Daddy, can I show Briony Sally's pups? I know she'll like them.'

Briony couldn't help the giggle, partly nervous in origin, that rose to her lips at the sight of Teale's face.

'Am I *never* to be alone with you?' he growled in a low voice for her ears only. And to Scott, 'Come on, then. But only a quick visit. Briony's got two hungry cats waiting for her.' He led the way out to the barn, where Sally had been allotted a cosy corner.

The pups, two dogs and two bitches, were as appealing as their mother, and Briony was as besotted over them as even Scott could have wished.

'They're adorable,' she crooned as she stood, Teale's arm about her waist, looking down at the little family.

'So are you,' Teale whispered, his breath fanning her ear. 'Just how soon am I going to be able to tell you *how* adorable?'

She looked up at him and met a gaze so ardent that her heart constricted in her breast.

'Oh, Teale, I *do* love you,' she said softly.

'Would you like Daddy to give you one of Sally's puppies?' Scott asked.

'They'll *all* belong to her, you little monster, if you ever give me a chance to propose to her,' Teale muttered so that only Briony could hear his words. Then, in a louder voice, he said to Scott, 'Come on! That's it! Back to the house. You're going to visit your Auntie Rhoda for the day.'

'For the *whole day*?' Briony said, deliberately demure.

'Or maybe longer,' Teale told her, love and laughter mingling in his dark eyes. 'Maybe he'd better pack his pyjamas!'

The drive into Gwinvercombe was not achieved easily. Though the snow ploughs had been out on the main roads, the winding country lanes were still treacherous. But Briony felt no fear; Teale's hands were sure and confident upon the wheel.

'You're very quiet,' he said when they had covered several miles in silence.

'Happily quiet,' she told him. 'Besides, I didn't want to distract you while you were driving.'

He risked a quick sideways smile, the smile that always had such an incredible effect on her senses.

'I admit you *are* a distraction,' he said and at his next words Briony was swamped with a flood of sensuous warmth, 'which is why I'm trying hard not to think about what's going to happen when I get you home.'

The cats, Tara and Stripey, were flatteringly glad to see them, arching their backs and entwining themselves about Briony's legs as she fed them. She sensed Teale's hard-held impatience as she returned their rapturous greetings, and a touch of coquettishness made her prolong her caresses. But at last she shut the kitchen door upon the animals and preceded him into the living-room. Suddenly, she felt absurdly nervous. She wandered about the room, straightening an ornament here, plumping up a cushion there.

'Briony!' he commanded from the depths of the couch. 'Stop fussing and come here. Unless,' huskily, 'you'd rather we went straight into the bedroom?'

'Oh, no!' she said quickly. That would seem too cold-blooded, too contrived. She didn't want the climax to their love to come until he had spoken to her of his love, coaxed her with kisses, seduced her with caresses. She wanted their progression to her bed to be a natural outcome of his lovemaking, reached only when desire had mounted too high to be any longer denied.

As she moved towards him, he reached out and entwined his arms about her waist, pulling her close so that his face was pressed against the softness of her stomach, and she felt his lips warm and seeking through the silky material of her suit. Through it, his hands sought and explored her yielding body until she knew a perfect delirium of sensation, until she longed for his touch upon her flesh, for all barriers to be removed.

He shared her sense of frustration.

'I could do without this thing,' he muttered. 'I want to feel your skin against my lips. Why do you have to wear something so difficult to remove?'

'When I put it on,' she reminded him, 'I didn't know I'd be seeing *you*.'

He gave a great shout of laughter and yanked her down across his lap.

'Am I to take it that if you *had* known you'd have worn something less inhibiting?' But he didn't wait for her indignant answer. His lips were already in possession of hers, while his fingers dealt expertly with the obstacle of which he complained.

'Briony, Briony,' he murmured between kisses, 'why was I ever such a fool as to think wanting meant only one thing? I *do* want you, and right now I admit *that's* the greatest need I have. But I've missed *you*, your company, the sound of your voice, your fine mind, your sense of humour. I've missed just *being* with you.' He held her a little away and looked into her face, flushed and bemused with happiness. 'Say you'll marry me, Briony! I want to hear you say it.'

'I really ought to make you go down on your knees and propose properly,' she teased.

'If that's what you want, I will.' He made as if to put her from him, but she wound her arms tightly about him, refusing to be dislodged.

'Just kiss me,' she whispered against his lips. 'Just go on kissing me, telling me you love me.'

This he proceeded to do very satisfactorily, not only his lips but his hands speaking of love, stirring her body with unerring sureness. At their tender insistence, she felt desire grow and expand until her demand became as active as his own, her fingers caressing the hard maleness of him.

He did not ask her this time but, taking her agreement for granted, he rose with her in his arms and moved toward the bedroom door, his lips never leaving hers. Gently he lowered her to the floor and slowly, making a worshipping ritual of it, he removed her scanty undergarments, his hands stroking and exploring what they revealed.

'You're so beautiful, my Briony,' he whispered against her breast. 'Let it always be this way between us. Don't ever hate me if sometimes I seem distant and abstracted. Even if you're not in my mind, you will always be in my heart. Don't let *us* ever grow apart?'

'Never,' she told him huskily. 'You'll write and I'll paint all the better for knowing we have this to look forward to at the end of the day.'

She lay naked on the bed, waiting for him to come to her, and saw the trembling of his hands, nervous with haste as he began to undress.

In the next room, the telephone began to ring.

'Ignore it!' he said. 'Nothing and nobody is going to come between us right now.' He shed the last of his garments and lowered himself beside her. Her body curved against him where it belonged, breast to breast, thigh to thigh, knowing the virility of him against her, knowing that he found their proximity as dizzily exciting as she did.

And the telephone continued to ring.

'It's no good,' she said desperately, 'we'll *have* to answer it. It must be urgent or they wouldn't go on ringing.'

'Oh, my God! There must be some conspiracy against my ever making love to you!' Teale rolled away from her and rose, pulling the quilt about him. '*I'll* answer it and get rid of whoever it is, and then we'll leave the damned thing off the hook!'

She smiled at his fervour, sharing his impatience. She stretched languorously as she waited eagerly for his return, for the splendour she knew his lovemaking would be. This surely must be what heaven was like, she thought, to know that Teale felt for her as she felt for him. She knew that no man had ever affected her as he did, stirring every nerve she possessed.

'Briony!' From the other room, his voice sounded harsh, unfamiliar. '*You'd* better take this!'

Reluctantly, she sat up and reached for her robe, a ridiculously diaphanous piece of material that scarcely concealed what it covered.

'What is it?' At the sight of his face, she caught her breath. It must be bad news of some kind to distort his features in that alarming way. Her first thought was that there had been an accident, but to whom? To Promilla, perhaps, now on her way home? She snatched the receiver from his grasp.

'Hello?'

'Mummy?' The voice was as clear as if Iseult had been in the next room instead of Provence. 'I called to wish you a happy New Year. Who was that man who answered? He sounded awfully grumpy.'

'Iseult, darling!' Relieved, Briony spoke with all the wealth of affection she felt for her daughter. 'Happy New Year! Did you have a lovely Christmas?'

'Yes, though I'm sorry I couldn't come and stay with you. But Daddy says I can come at Easter instead, if that's all right?'

'How *is* Daddy?' Briony enquired politely. 'Did he get home safely?' Jean-Luc had been to Australia on a business trip over Christmas. She turned towards Teale to give him an apologetic smile. But the beginnings of the smile were erased from her face as she saw his expression. 'Iseult, darling,' she said hastily, 'this call must be costing your grandparents a fortune. I'll write and I'll see you soon.'

Even so, it was two or three more agonising seconds before she was able to replace the receiver. She hurried into the bedroom to find Teale pulling on his trousers.

'Teale!' She ran to him, put her hands on his shoulders. 'What . . . ? Where are you going?'

'Where the hell do you think I'm going?' he demanded, shrugging off her touch. His face contorted with fury. 'Out of here as fast as I can.'

'But Teale...Oh, darling, surely we can talk about this? I...'

'There's nothing to talk about so far as I'm concerned. And don't call me darling.' His hands were shaking so much he could not do up the buttons of his shirt, and finally, with a savage gesture, he thrust the unfastened garment into the waistband of his trousers.

'Oh, my God!' She slumped down on to the bed, her heart-shaped face paled in horror. 'I was right! You *are* going to condemn me for...'

'Condemn you?' He was bitingly sarcastic. 'Too right I am. What did you expect?'

'Understanding!' she cried piteously. 'A little tolerance, perhaps, because you love me. Teale, I was only seventeen when...'

'Understanding, tolerance! Huh! You don't expect *much*, do you? No wonder you could speak so knowledgeably of marriage!' He dragged his sweater over his head.

'What are you talking about?' Dazedly, she stared at him.

'...marriage and its joys, its shared memories.'

'Marriage? But I'm...'

'No wonder you had such an amazing knack with children! How many have you?'

'Only one. Iseult. She...'

'My God, but you led me up the garden path, didn't you?' He flung himself into a chair to put on his socks and shoes.

'No, no!' She shook her head. 'Not deliberately. I...' But he was unstoppable in his anger.

'What? Not deliberately? Holding me at arm's length, giving me the come-on one minute, then playing hard to get, pretending outrage when I wanted to make love to you, preaching morality, spirituality, pretending you loved me...'

'I *do* love you, Teale!' She stood up and would have moved towards him, but he waved her away.

'Pretending to be holding out for marriage. Do you and your husband have some agreement?'

'I haven't got a...'

'Do you have an open marriage? I suppose *he* was the one staying here over Christmas?'

'No. I was...'

'A rapturous reunion, was it, while you parked your daughter on her grandparents?' He was on his feet now, striding about the room, beside himself with rage, shouting her down, drowning her attempted protests and explanations. 'And *did* he get home safely?'

'Teale, if you'd just *listen*!'

'Listen? To what? Lies? My God! To think I thought that this time I'd found a woman I could trust.'

'Teale! Oh, Teale, it isn't like that!' Briony was shaking from head to foot. Her mouth was dry with fear.

'No wonder you've always been so secretive about your past.'

'I wasn't secretive...' She'd been reserved but there had been good reason for that.

'You encouraged *me* to ramble on, baring my soul to you. Oh, you were very clever!'

'Teale, please let me explain. I meant to tell you about Iseult. But you were so scathing, so intolerant of promiscuity, I was afraid...'

'You meant to tell me about *Iseult*!' he mocked. 'I suppose her father was beside the point?'

'No, of course not. I would have...'

'Don't add lies to it, Briony.' He moved threateningly towards her. 'I'll give you one thing. You never actually lied, did you, until now? You just led me to believe things that were untrue.'

'No! No!' She shook her curly head vehemently.

He snatched at one of the imploring hands held out to him. 'You don't even wear a ring.'

'I don't *need* to wear a . . .'

'No? I suppose that would have cramped your style?' He threw the hand from him as though its touch might taint him.

He was fully dressed now. She *had* to get through to him before he slammed out of her life. As he moved towards the door, she stood between him and the only means of exit, and raised her voice to a shout, a thing she rarely did.

'*I am not married!*' And, more quietly, when she saw that at last she had riveted his attention, she repeated, 'Teale, I don't wear a ring, because I'm not married.'

'Not married?' They were standing almost toe to toe as he stared down at her. The angry colour had drained from his face, though a nerve still twitched violently in his cheek. 'Not married?' He said it as though he didn't understand the words.

'No!' Her blue eyes met his frankly, steadily. 'Not even divorced. I've never been married, Teale.'

'But you *do* have a child?' He seemed dazed now, bewildered, as though his recent anger had fogged his brain. 'She asked for you by name, called you her mother.'

'Yes,' she lifted her chin defiantly, 'I have a child. Iseult is ten years old now. Her father was a fellow student at art college. I was only seventeen when . . . I *would* have told you, Teale. I intended to tell you today, before we . . . But then we . . .' She blushed furiously and, for the first time in their long confrontation, her lids fluttered down.

'Why on earth didn't you tell me all this before?' He ran a hand around the back of his neck, his fingers massaging tense muscles.

'I *told* you why, only you wouldn't listen! Because of what you said once about your views on morality. I thought if we got to know each other first, you'd realise I'm not promiscuous, that that was the one and only mistake of my life. I'm not proud of it but,' defiantly, 'I wouldn't be without Iseult now. I love her.' Now that there was no need to bar his way, Briony moved away from the door, feeling she must sit down soon, before her legs gave way under her.

'But she doesn't live with you?' Teale followed her, not touching, but close, his eyes still on her averted face.

'No. When I gave her up two years ago, Jean-Luc had more to offer her than I could. It's a long story, but . . .'

'But we have all the time in the world for you to tell me.' His voice was so gentle now, so incredibly tender that she swung around and looked at him in disbelief.

'You mean . . . ?'

'I mean I'm sorry, my love.' He held out a hand but did not offer to touch her. 'Can you forgive me for my crass stupidity? I should have given you a chance to explain. But I just saw red. When I heard this child asking for *you* as her mother, mentioning her father in the same breath, I . . . Oh, God!' His shoulders sagged and he turned away. 'I thought I'd lost you—and just as I'd found you. Perhaps I *have* lost you now?'

'Then you're *not* shocked?' For the moment, Briony did not answer his implied question but continued to survey him doubtfully. 'About Iseult?' About . . . ?'

'About something that happened when you were scarcely more than a child yourself?' He groaned. 'What an intolerant prig you must have thought me all these months.' He slumped on to the side of the bed and covered his face with his hand. 'How could you possibly love me?'

'I do,' she said softly.

His head jerked up and he looked at her with dawning hope in his dark eyes.

'Still? In spite of everything I've said in the last ten minutes? I wouldn't blame you if you *hated* me.'

'I *love* you, Teale,' she repeated and, determined to convince him, she continued, 'I felt something the very first moment we met. Every time I saw you, I loved you more. But you were so sure love didn't exist, so determined never to marry again. Oh, Teale,' she moved hesitantly towards him, unsure of his reaction, placing her hands on his shoulders, 'those few weeks when I didn't see you, when I first thought even our friendship must end, because I had to save myself from further hurt— it was agony.' In a low voice that trembled slightly with the remembrance of what she had suffered, she told him, 'I was going to leave Gwinvercombe, go right away, as far away from you as I could.'

His hands grasped her waist and he drew her between his knees. He parted his lips to speak, but she put a finger lightly on his mouth.

'Let me tell you the whole of it . . . one more thing. In the end, I couldn't have gone. I love you so much, Teale,' her voice throbbed, 'that, last night, even when you hadn't asked me to marry you, I was going to give myself to you. I was going to settle for whatever you were prepared to give me. Anything would have been better than never seeing you again.'

'Oh, my love,' his voice was husky. 'I don't deserve you. I don't deserve to be loved like that. But believe me when I tell you, I drove back from London intending to ask you to marry me. Though why you should believe me,' he was bitterly self-condemnatory now, 'when *I* refused to believe in *you* . . .'

Tenderly, Briony drew his head against her breast. 'I *do* believe you. From now on, we'll always believe in each other.'

He would have pulled her closer still, but she freed herself and walked briskly towards the door.

'Briony!' His voice was taut. 'Where are you going?'

Over her shoulder, she cast him a demure look.

'To take that dratted phone off the hook.'

*   *   *

When she returned he was waiting for her, his clothes in a careless heap beside the bed.

'Is this thing supposed to preserve your modesty?' he asked huskily as he slid the almost transparent robe from her shoulders. 'Because let me tell you it's very unsuccessful and it has the most extraordinary effect on *me*.' As he drew her hard up against him, she believed him.

Muffled endearments were murmured against the curly thickness of her hair as he lifted her on to the bed. He lay still for a while, just crushing her against him, as if there were a world of satisfaction in just holding her. After their recent total mental and physical separation, it was almost enough for her too. Almost, but not quite. She shifted restlessly, wantonly against him.

Gradually his mouth began to move over her face, its exploration culminating in the searing fire of his kiss. The movements of his hands were so tantalisingly slow that she moaned softly in protest. Her own hands were locked about his neck, but now she let them move over him, exploring, glorying in his naked body, in the feel of smooth, warm skin, touching him, urging him to be more adventurous in his caresses.

Shivers of desire coursed down her spine as he complied.

'I love you, Teale,' she whispered with aching longing. 'I love you.'

'And I love you!' His breath came in shaking gasps, and this awareness of his need intensified her own. She longed for him to take her.

'Then *make* love to me!' she begged.

He moved swiftly then, his body covering her. A long, muscular leg parted hers. His hands arched her hips into him, and with the firm thrust of his strong thighs she felt the force of his manhood, its primitive desires unleashed within her. Its urgent, throbbing rhythm invaded the most intimate, thrilling recesses of her body. She responded to him with pulsating eagerness, the cres-

cendo building within her. She was oblivious now to
everything but the approach of pleasure, to the pleasure
she was giving him. Desire had erupted into passion,
passion that enfolded them in hungry, mindless abandon.
Together they soared, higher and higher, to shuddering
ecstasy as their bodies pulsed in consummation, in
mutual fulfilment.

She had no idea afterwards how long the sensations
had engulfed them. She lay curled against his side, his
arm under her neck, her body still molten with the fires
of his love. She murmured his name, and Teale turned
his head to look at her, his eyes two dark, burning coals.

'When I think of all the time I've wasted! But we won't
waste another moment, will we, my love?'

'Not a second,' she agreed. She reached out and ran
her fingers over the strong lineaments of his face, out-
lined the sensual mouth, traced the crooked bridge of
his nose. 'I've often wondered,' she told him, 'how you
broke your nose. Did somebody hit you?'

He grinned.

'Perhaps they should have done, frequently, over the
head. I might have come to my senses sooner. No, it's
much simpler than that. I used to play rugby in my mad
youth. And, speaking of mad youth——' he rolled over
to face her '—I feel more absurdly young than I have
in years. Younger and,' teasingly, 'more virile!' His tone
was teasing, but his eyes questioned her. Tentatively, he
touched her, his lips following his hands. He kissed each
breast, his lips burning. But he had no need to rekindle
her desire. Eagerly, she arched to meet him.

His lovemaking this time was as powerful but less
urgent, devoting more time to bringing her to even
greater heights of physical delight.

Much later, Briony awoke. The room was dark, but
the curtains were wide open, framing Teale against the
moonlight. His ears must have been alert for the slightest
sound, for as she stirred she saw him turn.

'Come here,' he said softly.

She slid from the bed and went to stand beside him, shivering slightly in the chill night air. He pointed beyond the window.

'Look at the sky,' he told her, his tone almost awed.

In the snow-filled sky, streaks of crimson flared fanlike, staining the sea to vermilion.

'If I painted a sky like that, no one would ever believe it!' Briony breathed.

'From now on,' Teale told her whimsically 'all our skies will be coloured red, the colour of love.' Then, 'Come back to bed, my love. You're cold...and,' throatily, 'the night isn't over yet.'

Conscience, scanda and desire.

A dynamic story of a woman whose integrity, both personal and professional, is compromised by the intrigue that surrounds her.

Against a background of corrupt Chinese government officials, the CIA and a high powered international art scandal, Lindsay Danner becomes the perfect pawn in a deadly game. Only ex-CIA hit man Catlin can ensure she succeeds... and lives.

Together they find a love which will unite them and overcome the impossible odds they face.

Available May. Price £3.50

W◉RLDWIDE

Available from Boots, Martins, John Menzies, W.H. Smith, Woolworths and other paperback stockists.

 **ROMANCE**

Next month's romances from Mills & Boon

Each month, you can choose from a world of variety in romance with Mills & Boon. These are the new titles to look out for next month.

SEND ME NO FLOWERS Katherine Arthur
ONE STOLEN MOMENT Rosemary Hammond
YOU CAN LOVE A STRANGER Charlotte Lamb
FALLING IN LOVE AGAIN Marjorie Lewty
UNEXPECTED INHERITANCE Margaret Mayo
EYE OF HEAVEN Michelle Reid
CATALAN CHRISTMAS Anne Weale
SATAN'S ISLAND Sally Wentworth
TOO LONG A SACRIFICE Yvonne Whittal
THE COUNT'S VENDETTA Sara Wood
JOURNEY OF DISCOVERY Jessica Marchant
A SURE INSTINCT Sally Stewart
CATCH A DREAM Celia Scott
DEVIL MOON Margaret Way

Buy them from your usual paperback stockist, or write to: Mills & Boon Reader Service, P.O. Box 236, Thornton Rd, Croydon, Surrey CR9 3RU, England. Readers in Southern Africa — write to: Independent Book Services Pty, Postbag X3010, Randburg, 2125, S. Africa.

Mills & Boon
the rose of romance

AND THEN HE KISSED HER...

This is the title of our new venture — an audio tape designed to help you become a successful Mills & Boon author!

In the past, those of you who asked us for advice on how to write for Mills & Boon have been supplied with brief printed guidelines. Our new tape expands on these and, by carefully chosen examples, shows you how to make your story come alive. And we think you'll enjoy listening to it.

You can still get the printed guidelines by writing to our Editorial Department. But, if you would like to have the tape, please send a cheque or postal order for £4.95 (which includes VAT and postage) to:

VAT REG. No. 232 4334 96

- -

AND THEN HE KISSED HER...

To: Mills & Boon Reader Service, FREEPOST, P.O. Box 236, Croydon, Surrey CR9 9EL.

Please send me _____ copies of the audio tape. I enclose a cheque/postal order*, crossed and made payable to Mills & Boon Reader Service, for the sum of £_____. *Please delete whichever is not applicable.

Signature _____

Name (BLOCK LETTERS) _____

Address _____

_____ Post Code _____

YOU MAY BE MAILED WITH OTHER OFFERS AS A RESULT OF THIS APPLICATION   ED1